In This Season
of Rage and Melancholy
Such Irrevocable Acts as These

MONGREL EMPIRE PRESS
NORMAN, OKLAHOMA, UNITED STATES OF AMERICA

2016

FIRST EDITION, 2016

**In This Season
of Rage and Melancholy
Such Irrevocable Acts as These**
© 2016 by Kat Meads

ISBN 978-0-9972517-4-6

Cover Art
© 2016 by Philip Rosenthal

Author Photo
Philip Rosenthal

MONGREL EMPIRE PRESS
NORMAN, OK

ONLINE CATALOGUE: WWW.MONGRELEMPIRE.ORG

This publisher is a proud member of

COUNCIL OF LITERARY MAGAZINES & PRESSES
w w w . c l m p . o r g

Book Design: Mongrel Empire Press using iWork Pages

In This Season
of Rage and Melancholy
Such Irrevocable Acts as These

Kat Meads

Sections of this novel first appeared in *Catamaran Literary Reader* and *WIPs: Works (of Fiction) in Progress.*

For the farmers, Meads and Sears

We can never cease to be ourselves.

—Joseph Conrad

* * *

Typically, He came with the dark.

Black eyes, sharp nose. Slicked-back hair that glistened. Elegant, vain, detached. Contemptuous of the quantity and quality of endless petitions foisted upon Him. Dismissive of effort. Indifferent to struggle. Insolent. Glamorous, in a late-night, end-of-the-world, cynical sort of way.

Beth dressed her deity in a tux, had Him speak with a foreign accent because she wanted Him to sound like no one else she knew, to resemble in no fashion the God who came before.

Her creation had no use for the Pentecostal "dance."

The flailing, the writhing, the speaking in tongues.

"Dreadful choreography," He denounced. "Appallingly acted. A dismal production, start to finish."

Her version wore pointy shoes—also black. More often than not, while visiting, He crossed his legs. Always He smoked. The cigarette holder had been an afterthought but now she couldn't imagine Him without the prop. He came with His own stage set, one that overlaid a corner of her shabby trailer. Potted palms. A round café table of silver chrome and black enamel. A floor of black and white tiles that slanted away from Him, toward her. And in the background, the deep, deep background, music provided by a band dedicated to swing.

Because she believed He was her fantasy to do with as she pleased, she also assumed He could be dismissed. The day or, rather, the night she tired of His company—poof, He'd vanish. But when that night arrived and she'd drunk herself drunk enough to bid Him farewell, He laughed, teeth glinting along with His shoes.

"Dearest darling Elizabeth," He chided. "Aspire not to be ridiculous. For both our sakes."

Only He called her Elizabeth.

Her fault. She'd wanted to avoid Pentecostal chumminess, the Pentecostal assumption of familiarity, earned or unearned. Now: no going back. Now He refused to call her anything else. And now she knew what she hadn't known in advance: mockery and her birth name fit hand in glove.

1

Tonight He'd arrived without commotion, seemed content to watch and smoke and sneer in silence. Once, twice, she managed to forget He was there at all, straining His patience. When at last He deigned to speak, He skipped the preliminaries, repeated Himself for emphasis.

"Elizabeth, the ridiculous. Ridiculous Elizabeth."

Aspiring to appear less so, she drank steadily. And then she slipped, must have slipped, from the trailer's come-with couch onto its come-with carpet, spilling beer. And there she must have stayed, damp with beer, hours passing, for when next she opened her eyes she truly was alone.

Because it was daylight.

Because she had, again, disgusted God.

ONE

"Mickey? They're starting to arrive."

His eyes were as good as Becca's. He saw the fucking lineup. Car after car winding between pines and the rare oak, heading for his brick driveway. A guest list that mixed and mingled local ass kissers and shit-heel lickers with a discreet number of out-of-town investors whose asses he'd have to kiss in order to offload another chunk of county. Another afternoon spent with fake buddies and sentimental drunks.

"And what will my liquor be washing down today?"

"Oysters, scallops and shrimp for the Yanks. Barbecue and ribs for the sheriff and deputies," Becca counted off.

"And for dessert?"

"The opportunity to invest in Waterman Enterprises."

"For the chosen few."

"For anyone who comes up with the cash," Becca corrected.

"So we're set up out by the pool?"

"With a second spread inside."

He felt her behind him, waiting.

"Mickey?"

"What?"

"Don't blow this one off. It's important."

"So you've said."

"And meant."

"Lay off, Becca. I know the drill."

"They'll be wondering where you are."

"Not after they've located bar one or two."

"Walk back with me."

To the stark and sterile white-brick ranch, she meant. The showpiece he'd built on Oak Park Colony's primo lot. The "entertainment pad" with the oblong pool around which caterers currently scurried and ice sculptures melted and the fumes of roasting pig rose and hovered. The house befitting the junior Mickey Waterman, real estate developer, county power broker, fucking budding politician.

"Don't hide out here. Not today."

He turned.

5

"Hide out in my spawning hole? No, you think not, Becca? Not today? Why the fuck not today?"

Since today, like any day, like some portion of every day, forced him back to this rotting farmhouse to gaze upon pig troughs and barbed wire and kudzu, the rusted-out Ford on blocks, the hardwood mantel he'd mutilated as a substitute for carving up Mickey Senior's bones. Because if he *neglected* this daily dose of in-the-face and nose and gut reminders he might *forget* that having a son of a bitch daddy locked in a coffin eliminated just one of a stream of sons of bitches in Mawatuck County ready, eager, and able to kick Mickey Junior in the nuts.

"Remember that contractor? Insisted I raze the…what did he call it? 'The eyesore.'"

"I wasn't part of that meeting," Becca said.

And didn't want to hear a replay—but fuck that. She could stick her fingers in her ears for all he cared.

"Yeah, *eyesore*—that's what he said. Then he said: 'It'll ruin your view, Mr. Waterman.' And I said: 'I like the eyesore view.' And he said: 'But, but, Mr. Waterman.' And I said: 'Bulldoze an inch, Mr. But But, and you'll never work in this county again.'"

"Because what's persuasion without threat?" Becca asked, pretending to play along but not pretending very fucking hard.

"Quit looking at your watch."

"Can't," she said.

"Won't," he said.

"We need to go, Mickey."

"Not before I finish telling my story."

"What's left to tell?"

"The most important part: response to threat."

"Which was?"

He looked out the window.

"'Yessir, yessir, yessir, Mr. Waterman. Whatever you say, whatever you say.'"

"Fear, the motivator," Becca said.

"You got that fucking right."

"So now can we go?"

At night in this house, scratching his pimples, he'd listen to Mickey Senior snore in the bedroom beneath his own, trying, through sheer force of will, to turn that noisy sleep permanent. Night and day, he hoped Senior would fall into the river, step in front of a speeding car, die by any means natural or foul, just get the fuck out of his life. It hadn't happened soon enough, but when that fat heart finally did explode, he didn't pretend to be sorry.

No fucking way.

"The best of the best of the bastards, Becca? You know what makes them the best?"

"I have my theories," she said.

"Weaned on fucking fear themselves. Familiar with the receiving end of that game. So: their turn in the big leagues? They've got both ends covered."

"Fascinating. Why not share those insights with our lovely guests?"

"Maybe I will."

"Then we're off," Becca said.

"What's the rush? None of those shits are leaving anytime soon."

"You can't be sure of that."

"The fuck I can't."

"Mickey…"

"Remember the hunting lodge near Carson's Inlet? Down at the marshy end?"

"We don't have time for more reminiscing."

He turned again to face her.

"If I say we have the fucking time, we have the fucking time. And not even you get to tell me otherwise."

"Then I *strongly suggest* we dispense with the reminiscing," she said.

Tough-nut Becca. Not the least bit afraid of him or any other bastard.

The last person Daddy Mick wanted hanging around the hunting lodge was his bowlegged kid. But there Mickey Junior was all the same, hiding in the marshes, watching Senior's guests porch-sit in November, drinking cocktails like it was summertime, staying put in that damp chill to prove their Northern balls were cold-tested, cold-immune, that no dumb-fuck Cracker dumping sugar in his whiskey could outlast them on his Cracker porch.

On a regular basis, Mickey the kid got as close to that sit-off as he dared. Then came the twilight one of those drunk Yanks decided to take a piss. Since he couldn't crawl fast enough through mud and chest-high reeds to get out of range, he got seen, pegged for a white trash half-breed hungering for a look at Massa Mickey's mansion. Finished pissing, the Yank flipped him a quarter, indifferent to whether that North-tainted coin was scooped up or pissed on in turn. No stooge, yeah, he'd grabbed the money. He'd also on-the-spot vowed to repay the insult—and had, many times over, selling Yanks Mawatuck swampland.

But paying back Mickey Senior?

Never-ending proposition.

Getting even with a dead man took some of the fun out of it—but enough to stop? Not even close. He'd be paying back Daddy Mick until he was a corpse himself. And if one corpse could bedevil another, he'd keep at it.

Ever after.

Without pause.

Every Mawatuck Cracker with a roof over his head mocked the house where Senior parked his family, but no one mocked the spare-no-expense-tricked-out hunting lodge built to woo distributors, expand the market for Waterman strawberries, cantaloupes and peaches.

Business decision, son.

Ducks, beds, meals and liquor those buyers got—but not for free. Once his guests were tanked up and isolated on his land, Senior liked to tell stories about that rare white citizen of the New South, 1959, who went out of his way to hire blacks over whites.

Captive audience, man.

And that captive audience nodded, refilled their glasses, relit their cigars. They'd bagged five ducks apiece, were high on the fool's booze. Why not let Big Daddy Doofus brag on himself? What the fuck did they care what kind of bullshit he spouted?

And it was bullshit. The ripest.

Senior hired migrant blacks over whites for one reason and one reason only: their labor came cheapest.

Fuck equality.

Fuck justice.

Hell, I'd hire me a busload of chartreuse pickers if they saved me a dime.

Proud of that stinginess. Dirt-proud.

Waterman migrant camps fended off none of the elements: heat, rain, mosquitoes, vipers. The cabins had no front doors, no running water, no electricity. Need a toilet? Take your pick: woods or ditch.

A couple of times he'd sneaked over to shoot marbles with the left-behinds—kids too young or scrawny to pick their weight in produce. Got away with it once, not twice. Gathered around a dirt circle, he and black boys throwing snake eyes, spit happy until they heard someone coming. A fucking big someone.

Since he didn't know their daddies, he figured they didn't know his, but they recognized a mad white man bearing down when they saw one. Scattered like buck shot, his playmates, leaving him to his fate.

Every peephole in the camp had a view of his bare whipped ass and weeper's snot. Every peephole.

"You come to this camp again, you ain't gonna have a tail left to beat. You understand me, boy?"

Understand? Fuck no. But he knew better than to argue crouched beneath a belly big enough to block the sun.

Proud of his fat too, Daddy Mick.

A fat man's a successful man. Ain't you realized that yet, boy? This belly of mine is prosperity in the round.

Competed in every feed-your-face contest the county put on, Senior did. Shoveled down whatever meat or sweets the bakers of Mawatuck piled on his plate.

Prize-winning gluttony.

Blue ribbons for refusing to push back from the table, take that obscenely jiggling belly elsewhere.

Hell, I could get so fat I'd have to wear a feed sack and folks around here would still bow and scrape.

But it wasn't Daddy Mick, it was Mama Myra who wore the equivalent of feed sacks. Never replaced, never updated, the same shapeless, washed-thin housedresses to bag produce, slop hogs, hoof it to church.

Walked the mile and a half to Mawatuck Baptist because her pinchpenny husband said: *Mile and a half one way, Myra? Not worth burning gasoline for. You want to visit your Lord's house, he gave you the feet to manage.*

Never objected, never retaliated with her tongue or a butcher knife. Just set off down the road, giving every other Mawatuck churchgoer chance to pity and gloat.

Myra Waterman walking when Mickey Senior's got all that money. Ain't that a pitiful sight? Ain't it, though?

Mama Myra trekking for salvation, Daddy Mick gobbling down breakfast, Mickey Junior swearing vengeance. That's how the Waterman clan spent their Sundays. And every Sunday and every day between Sundays, the kid he was then promised himself and un-listening Mawatuck: *Wait till the next Waterman's in charge. Then we'll see who's fucking pitiful. Then you'll all fucking see.*

Mickey entered the master bedroom through a back door designed for unobserved entrances and exits. There were flecks of dirt on the cuffs of his slacks, probably flecks of ancient pig shit.

A hotshot like Mickey Waterman Junior couldn't be seen with grubby cuffs, now fucking could he?

On the plush carpet of a bedroom four times the size of any of Senior's rooms, he dropped his pants. Stepped into a wall-length closet. Had his pick of Italian suits, silk shirts, loafers soft and softer. Nothing stacked, folded, hung or lined up in that collection of Becca-selected fashions gave away a greaseball past or smacked of hood.

Almost nothing.

"I'm keeping the fucking jacket, Becca."

Elbows nicked, shoulder seams already unraveling when he snatched it off the rack of a Ward Street pawnshop. But he needed that battered leather coat, still needed it—for the incentive. Alone in this echo-pit of a house, he slipped it on, pushed his fists through threaded lining, rattled around the bedroom, the bar, wore it to squat by the pool, howl at the fucking moon—whatever. But before taking it off, he made sure to bury his nose in the jacket's armpits and breathe in the stench of the cash-poor desperate.

Whatever he had to do to keep from being and smelling that desperate again, he'd do, including hosting these fucking parties.

Clinking glasses, clattering silverware, hyena laughs. He wasn't particularly missed. Becca could handle a busload of Yahoos and Yankees by herself. Pitch them hard, take their money. She didn't need his sales help at these gatherings and he didn't give it—not directly. Instead he circulated, watching and waiting for guests to grope a server's boob, yodel "Whiter Shade of Pale," puke in the bushes, gossip about the latest "strapped for cash" landowner experiencing "hard times" in Mawatuck County.

"It's not that I'm *against* taking advantage of indiscretions," Becca said. "But realize: there are risks to the practice."

Calculating pluses and minuses: a Becca specialty. And why wouldn't it be? For anyone who'd climbed her way out of heritage that assumed she was only as good as her cunt, who learned the art of keeping books straight, then crooked, playing the percentages made sense. But he wasn't Becca. If he ran wailing from every risk, passed on every wildcard gamble, the boredom would kill him before nature could.

Stay alive to stay bored? Why the fuck bother?

In the bathroom sink—one of them—he rinsed his hands, dabbed at his hair, a bathtub behind him big enough to float a whale the size of Senior.

One hamburger a day, he'd allowed himself, ages ten through twelve, and not a swallow more. Thirteenth birthday, he'd wrapped his mama's sewing tape around his waist, recorded the number and every month thereafter measured and compared. If the tape pulled, if he had any trouble whatsoever reaching his belt hole of choice, he skipped that day's meal. As further safeguard, in high school, he bought his jeans, his sparkle and spangle shirts, even his elevated boots, two sizes too small. He looked scrawny, puny, wasted, and that was the way he wanted to look. Not an inch of fat or bloat anywhere.

The Mickey facing him now?

Who was he?

Teeth capped, acne free. Fluffy, layered hair.

"No, really, it's good," Becca insisted. "It looks like the hair of someone more interested in a mirror than money."

Fooling a mirror—the first step in fooling the world.

To fool Mawatuck, he'd had to give up the tattoos as well as the pompadour.

"Are you sure you want to go through with this?" Miss Blonde Technician had asked in a pristine office stocked with antiseptics.

Idiot.

He was there, wasn't he?

He'd rolled up his sleeve, hadn't he?

"Just do it!"

The same words he'd screamed at the scumbag Ward Street tattooist who'd inked it in.

"You know this is going to hurt like bejesus, right?" that toothless codger warned, naked light bulb swinging above their heads, one needle for all.

And it had. But if necessary he'd have chewed glass to get that snake and staff laid into his flesh. Loved that fucking tattoo, man. Loved it and wore it proudly. Nothing short of daddy vengeance could have separated him from it, and nothing short of daddy vengeance had.

As soon as Mickey stepped foot in sunlight, Becca saw him—Becca always saw him before anyone else. The gimp she was chatting up? Not a clue he'd lost the attention of the petite flatterer with the high, tight butt.

In between shindigs, he forgot how tiny Becca looked, crammed among beefy men.

Shrimps, the both of them.

Highly effective shrimps.

Now, as a team, they'd work the joint.

Most of Mawatuck assumed Waterman Enterprises had no repeat customers, which was far, far from being the case. They had clients they'd ripped off repeatedly and still couldn't beat off with a pitchfork.

With Oak Park Colony, they'd advertised pretty much what they'd sold: flat, sunny parcels. Although building sites that included an actual oak tree were few and far between, there were plenty of pines to block the sky. For building lots with water access, the safeguard of bulkheading was left to the buyer's discretion—and expense. Not part of the list price. New owners who ignored the shoring up process soon found themselves with considerably less property than was officially stated on their deed.

Erosion.

Blame Mother Nature.

Not the fault of Waterman Enterprises.

Not a winnable lawsuit.

Read the fucking contract.

To move the lowland properties of Oak Park Extension, he and Becca had prepared to sell more "creatively." Not much of that required to date. Lots had been and were selling briskly. And if original investors became disgruntled and resold? If the gouged turned around and gouged the next in line? What did he care? He'd already pocketed his bundle.

"Mickey, son."

Mawatuck's recently elected sheriff hurried over to extend a pulpy hand.

Without Waterman backing, Titus Morris wouldn't have a badge, much less a posse.

"Glad you could make it, Titus."

"Wouldn't miss it for the world, son. You throw a helluva party."

The "son" was pure affectation. Titus Morris was a year younger than he was.

"Help yourself to a plate of ribs, Titus. No need to stand on ceremony."

"Heading that way directly, but first I need me a juice refill. This glass hardly holds a thimbleful."

Mawatuck's sheriff was welcome to all the Waterman whiskey he could pour down his gullet because drink had gotten Titus owned.

"Bring a bottle," Mickey instructed the waitress. "The sheriff's dry, drink-wise."

A pointed reference and one understood.

As a mere sheriff's deputy, at a previous Waterman bash, Titus Morris had drunk many thimblefuls of whiskey. Sober, Titus had a loud mouth. It got louder, the more he drank. When the deputy's "mighty white of ya" exclamations began to rise and carry, Becca positioned herself to create a diversion. He'd signaled to let it play. Soon thereafter he'd felt a whoosh of air, looked down to see his loafers splotchy with chlorinated drops and Titus slapping at pool water.

The Yank beside him, breath as whiskey-doused as the man in chlorine, said: "True son of the South—eh, Mick?"

He'd lifted his eyebrows, smiled, both he and Becca rapidly tallying reactions: the smug, the disgusted, the delighted.

"And to think you actually live here," continued the asshole at his side.

"A wonder, isn't it?" he'd replied before picking up a towel.

"Didn't see that drop off, sure didn't," Titus had blathered, led past Yanks reaffirmed in their belief that all Southerners were morons, hence no Southerner was capable of putting together a deal that bested their kind.

Titus's dip had kept Becca scurrying for the remainder of the party. By its conclusion they'd unloaded the last of the Oak Park Colony lots, prompting Becca to suggest they pay a deputy to fall into the pool at every party.

For the deputy named Titus, he'd had other plans. During that relatively early stage of operations, they'd yet to secure a reliable friend in the Sheriff's Department.

While the deputy's clothes spun in the dryer, he'd kept the deputy-in-a-towel company, one of a series of Waterman courtesies that came with strings attached. "Encouraged" to run for sheriff, Titus ran and—backed by Waterman funds—won. Whether or not they found themselves in need of a Mawatuck sheriff's personalized service and/or intervention, they had now acquired sheriff insurance. Insurance made Becca happy; insurance improved their odds.

But a Waterman pawn—wet, dry, drunk or sober—held little entertainment value. The sheriff's red face and squirrelly deference had begun to bore him beyond his boredom tolerance.

"Enjoy yourself, Titus," he said before moving on.

At the interior bar he poured two fingers of whiskey into his own glass, an amount he'd nurse throughout the afternoon.

"Is everything satisfactory, Mr. Waterman?"

Another someone anxious to please, the bulk of her income derived from catering the parties of Mickey Waterman.

"Yes. Very nice. You've checked with Ms. Denby?"

"Yes sir. We moved the bar closer to the pool, as she requested."

Fucking Becca.

Prepping the scene.

He looked past the pool's clear waters toward the river's murky brown line, marveling yet again that so many people wanted to live near or next to what looked to his eye like a stream of liquid shit.

The placard in the grass he'd missed.

Until now.

Becca touched his elbow.

"Like it?"

"You're rushing things."

"Not at all," she said.

Mickey Waterman, Commissioner—shaded by a mimosa tree.

"Comma's a nice touch."

"Isn't it? As if the election had already come and gone, victory a fact," she said.

And victory was a fact—Becca would make sure of it. They might go about their getting a little differently, he and Becca, but when she swore "done," done it was.

Watch and learn, saps.

Men who bet against Becca lost their shirts.

In his closet: no shortage of shirts.

Two

It was a tradition. Beth spent every Friday night drinking with George and Leeta in George and Leeta's half beige, half yellow kitchen. The yellow had been her idea.

Painting day, she'd supplied one paint can, two brushes and three six-packs. Working together, she and Leeta had barely finished one wall before Leeta quit and threw her brush out the back door.

"Why bother? Yellow, green or black, a dump still looks like a dump."

"Come on, Leeta," she'd begged then. "Come on."

"Knock yourself out, pal. This girl's done."

With painting. Not with drinking or complaining about cracked floorboards, flaking ceilings, doors that wouldn't shut, faucets that dripped and what Leeta called "crappier than crap furniture," donated by George's relatives.

It had been George's house before it was George and Leeta's house. And before it had been George's house, it had been his dad's.

"We'd live better if we lived in a tent," Leeta griped.

When George was around and Leeta started bitching about the house, he always said: "Tell her, Lizzie Beth. Remind your good buddy what a fine house she comes home to everyday. Fields on three sides and bonus sheds."

Despite the leaky faucets and water-ringed furniture and partially painted walls, Beth agreed with George. It was a fine house. Anywhere George and Leeta lived would be a fine house.

From the front door, this Friday evening, Beth followed a trail of Leeta's "slave labor clothes" to the kitchen.

"Strip on your way to the refrigerator?" she asked.

In a slip Leeta sat at the kitchen table.

"This house gets hot as hell closed up all day."

The tomatoes spilling out of Leeta's sandwich were only slightly redder than the hair on Leeta's head—the hair on Leeta's head *this* week.

A longtime red fan, Leeta. If Beth had supplied red paint back when, would they have finished the painting job?

"Want a sandwich?"

"No thanks."

"George didn't grow the tomatoes, if that's what's holding you back."

It wasn't. She opened a beer.

"So what incredibly exciting things happened at Mawatuck Savings this week? Feel free to invent."

To work as a bank teller at Mawatuck Savings, Beth drove five miles, round trip. To work as a receptionist at Bevin General, Leeta crossed county lines. Stopped for speeding, Leeta usually succeeded in talking her way out of ticket.

"You know how? By asking: 'Do I look like someone in a hurry to get to work?'"

When Leeta was high, she did a wicked, wicked candy striper imitation and claimed she could sing "Abide with Me" backwards having heard the "forward version at least a million times," thanks to the hospital chapel's soundtrack.

No matter how drunk, Beth never encouraged Leeta to sing "Abide with Me" backwards. Hymns were hymns. Dangerous territory.

"Not much to tell. This was my week to work the drive-through window."

From her high-rise teller stool, privy to the back seats, front seats, dashboards and floorboards of cars, Beth saw wadded Kleenex, dirty socks, crushed newspapers, tangled tape, tooth-marked pizza, bottles of Metamucil, boxes of tampons.

It told too much, that view. Told on.

"And Bevin General? Things hopping over there?"

Leeta shrugged. "Stella Wallace's mother kicked off."

"When?"

"Fifteen minutes after a rose delivery. And not one of the hospital coffee shop's wilt-y arrangements either. FTD."

"From Stella?"

"From brother Sonny, so Stella said. Then she tells me: 'Oh Leeta, my mama was such a saint!' And I said: 'Same saint that beat you black and blue?'"

"You did not."

"No, but I sure as hell should have. Why be nice? Stella accused me of trying to fuck my way to Homecoming Queen. Remember?"

Of course Beth remembered.

Between biology class and study hall, Stella Wallace had stormed into the girls' bathroom, fight ready. At the time, she'd been peeing; Leeta, reapplying eye shadow.

Stella opened with: "Fuck every vote you got, slut?"

"I most certainly did," Leeta said—to drive Stella nuttier. "Sorry that scheme didn't work as well for you. Ten votes total. Guess you should have started earlier."

"Wouldn't want something I had to screw to get," Stella declared.

Leeta grinned. "Sure about that?"

"Yeah I'm sure!" Stella insisted, sounding anything but.

Not that it mattered one way or the other by then. Stella and Leeta had both lost out to Rebecca Denby. Crowned at halftime on the football field, skinny everywhere but her middle, Queen Becca had looked... determined.

In the girls' bathroom, Leeta said: "Save it, Stella. You would have rolled the janitor to win."

Not only was Leeta Porter *filth*, not only was Leeta Porter a *slut*, Leeta Porter didn't *deserve* George Scaff. "He's not the fool you take him for," Stella announced.

"Who says I take him for a fool, Stella?"

"One of these days he's going to wise up and leave your sorry ass."

Which was when Beth had slammed out of the stall, smacking her knee.

"Never!" she'd declared in defense of George, in defense of George and Leeta.

Which had made Leeta laugh at *her*, the defender.

"Calm down, cowgirl. I can handle this. Stella fights worse than she fucks."

This evening, in Leeta's kitchen, a piece of tomato peel had wedged between two of Leeta's front teeth. The extra bit of red didn't make Leeta seem any fiercer, any more of a threat to enemies, but it did make Leeta look like Leeta.

Leeta often had clotted teeth.

"Will Sonny come home for the funeral?"

"Why would he? Mom's not gonna know the difference."

"Still."

"Still what?" Leeta scoffed. "I'll give Sonny Wallace this: wanted to get the hell out of Mawatuck, got the hell out, never looked back."

They heard George smacking his cap against his jeans before they saw his grinning face.

"What's this, ladies? Started the fun without me?"

A horse fly came in the house with him.

Since Leeta's lips were locked in a pout, Beth answered.

"Nope. Haven't gotten to the fun, still concentrating on the drinks."

21

Bending, George nuzzled Leeta's neck.

"Thanks a lot! Now I'm coated with dirt."

"Nothing wrong with dirt, wifey. Dirt's a good thing."

"Yeah, and if we waited for you to finish rolling in it, we'd never get drunk," Leeta fussed.

"Seriously doubt that," he said, still grinning.

"Fuck you," Leeta said.

"Has been and hope it always will be my pleasure to fuck you, darlin'," George said, reaching for a beer.

And just like that, in Leeta and George's half-beige/half-yellow kitchen halfway through an ordinary Friday night, Beth teared up, trembled.

Because of a silly, wonderful, cast-off remark, husband to wife.

Because George loved—still loved—Leeta.

How Jerry Banks discovered her secret Beth never found out. But he'd discovered it, second grade.

On the playground he'd cornered her.

"Roll, Holy Roller. Roll."

Counting on Jerry's limited attention span, she'd submitted to the arm wrenching. Then his pals joined in, tossing bits of gravel and oyster shell at her. She hadn't—for long—worried about being injured by Jerry's backup team. Inexpert marksmen, the bunch. Repeatedly they threw wide of the mark.

Jerry was and remained her prime concern. Boys showing off for other boys lost what conscience they had.

As the pain shot from her wrist to her shoulder, to prevent begging for release, she bit down hard on her tongue. It lasted as long as it lasted: Jerry's insistence, her resistance. Then it was over. When Jerry lost focus, went elsewhere, her arm hurt but wasn't broken. She was on her knees but hadn't torn her dress. All in all, it seemed a victory.

In the wake of that initial hazing, she'd assumed she'd lost entertainment value for Jerry and pals. Mostly she had. Mostly she got to ride the giant strides and merry-go-round, jump rope and play jacks like everybody else. But if she made the mistake of straying too far from the pack, Jerry's pack circled in.

The day Leeta happened upon their knot of tension, she'd eaten grit but still hadn't rolled.

"Hey!" Leeta shouted, ponytail twisted, shoes already scuffed. "Cut that out!"

When Jerry ignored the order, Leeta leapt onto his back and started kicking. To free himself from Leeta, Jerry had to let go of the Holy Roller.

Jerry fought dirty, but not nearly as dirty as Leeta. Before Jerry could get hold of Leeta's ponytail, she spat a wad that landed just north of his mouth. He grabbed his attacker by the throat; Leeta kept swinging, punching. For a long moment they separated, circled each other. Then he pushed and Leeta fell, but not before shrieking "teacher!" He had to check the bluff; they all did except Leeta, who jumped up and charged again. Once Leeta was on top of Jerry, the advantage was all hers; she outweighed him by at least ten pounds. Pinning his arms with her knees freed her hands to pinch his ears.

"Give," Leeta demanded.

He jerked his head no, girl fingers still attached to his earlobes.

"This minute!" Leeta warned, pinching harder.

And then, in an act of extraordinary bravery, Leeta leaned in and sank her teeth into Jerry's cheek.

Certifiably wounded, he yelped and surrendered.

After brushing off her socks and realigning her ponytail, Leeta set off for the water fountain. Like a sheepdog following its master, Beth trailed behind.

"You don't have to thank me," Leeta insisted, dribbling water. "I love to fight."

Leeta never asked and she never told why Jerry Banks expected her to roll—not at the water fountain that day or anywhere, anytime since. But the night of Leeta's rescue, Beth prayed hard to her Holy Roller God.

Please let Leeta Porter be my friend. Forever and ever. No matter what, no matter what.

For a God who could do anything, it seemed a minor request.

As a trio George and Beth and Leeta shifted kitchen to living room, Leeta kicking her work clothes out of the way.

"So Beth won't trip and maim herself."

A prediction far from farfetched. Rising from the kitchen chair, Beth felt a wee bit wobbly. Crossing into the living room, she dinged her shoulder on the doorframe.

"Looks like we'd better widen the doorway too," Leeta declared. "I'll get the chainsaw."

"And leave the termites nothing to do? Can't sanction it, darlin'," George said, straight-faced.

Leeta punched him, then relented. "Yeah. Okay. Why spoil a termite's fun?"

It was George who decided they should watch TV.

"Then you're in charge of the rabbit ears," Leeta ordered.

He yanked the antenna up; he yanked the antenna down. He jimmied it in every direction.

Nothing on the screen resembled people. Or cars or boats or houses or trees. Or dogs or cats or termites. To Beth, it looked like a box of gray fuzz.

"Can you make anything out?" she quizzed Leeta.

Maybe only she couldn't see what was what.

"Hell no," Leeta answered and threw one of George's brogans at the set.

George ducked sideways.

"Easy, slugger."

"I meant to hit the TV and that's what I hit!" Leeta crowed.

The picture did seem clearer.

Arms raised in victory, Leeta bounded up. Still on the couch, Beth and her beer counter-bounced. After applauding herself, Leeta slapped George's butt. Then they all resettled, a couch line of three.

For a while Beth attempted to follow the televised action. Then she didn't.

"Lizzie Beth's bored," George announced. "She'd rather build a beer can fort."

"Or a palace."

"Shush. Both of you." Leeta bent forward, squinting. "Is that cop supposed to be on the take?"

"The guy's a cop? Did not know that," George said.

"Corrupt at the moment but thinking about repenting," Beth said.

Repenting

Why had she used that word? She'd hardly been watching.

"Or you know," she fumbled, mumbled, on. "Admit the error of his ways."

"It's a cop show, Beth, not a fucking prayer meeting," Leeta said.

When Beth stood, she swayed, caught the edge of the coffee table with her knee. To reach the front door she had to navigate an obstacle course of empty, rolling beer cans.

"You're leaving *now*?" Leeta protested. "Shock Theatre's about to come on!"

"You'll have to be shocked without me."

George got to the door before she did.

"How about we ride together to the game tomorrow?" he suggested. "We'll swing by the trailer, pick you up."

"No thanks."

"Don't waste your breath, George. Queen Beth's in a snit. When Queen Beth's in a snit, she won't agree to anything."

"I'm not in a snit, Lee-ta," she said.

But she did feel drunk.

Out in the yard, George pointed out the Big Dipper, then Leo, the Lion. To get a better look at the sky, she leaned back, lost her balance, fell and kept falling until damp night grass stopped her.

Leeta and George, one on either side, pulled her up.

"Sleep here tonight," Leeta said.

"Nope."

"Why not? One night on our couch won't put you in traction."

"The trailer awaits."

"The trailer will be there tomorrow," George said.

"Maybe not. It's got tires."

Semi-deflated tires. Tires that hadn't spun round in years, but tires all the same.

She made it to and into the Plymouth—along with part of Leeta.

"Kindly get your head out of the window."

"I'd feel better if you stayed," Leeta said, trying to snatch the keys.

"And I'd feel better if I go. My vote's the tiebreaker."

"No tie. Two against one," Leeta insisted.

"But I'm the one holding the keys."

"Give 'em here, then."

Now the fingers dragging on her arm were sticky wet. Crossed, Leeta had resorted to biting her nails.

"George! A little help here!" Leeta called.

Punching the key toward the ignition switch, she missed.

"I make a mean cup of morning coffee, Lizzie Beth," George bribed.

"So do I. Leeta, get your head out."

"Then call when you get home, okay? Will you do that? Will you?"

"Bye, bye, Leeta. Bye, bye, George."

Backing out, she didn't flatten the driveway reflector but the Plymouth's fender did clip a corner shrub.

In the moony yard, leaning against each other, George and Leeta looked like one person instead of two.

She turned the wheel; the Plymouth shot forward on Highway 178.

A passenger coalesced.

"Such a lovely evening. How could you bear to tear yourself away?"

A bad night: when the tuxedo joined her outside the trailer, on the road. When He appeared, riding shotgun, she automatically accelerated to scare Him off, scare Him elsewhere.

But God was God. He stayed where He wanted to stay.

Tonight, in the passenger seat of her Plymouth, the tuxedo stayed put.

The pounding woke her.

Leeta, Beth guessed.

No one smacked a door quite like Leeta.

"I HEAR you!" she called to her instant regret.

If she'd kept her mouth shut, Leeta might have given up.

Who was she kidding? Leeta never gave up.

She'd taken off her jeans but nothing else to crash on the trailer's couch. During the night the t-shirt had bunched around her ribs like a ruffle.

Had she dreamed of ruffles?

"Elizabeth Jane Anderson! Open the goddamn door!"

Because it was Leeta, just Leeta, she didn't bother putting the jeans back on.

As soon as she twisted the lock, she started to sneeze.

Leeta had no sympathy, no pity.

"Serves you right, living in the middle of a cornfield."

She'd rented the trailer because it sat in the middle of a cornfield—not despite. Anyone who came looking for her had to, first, know the way. When the corn was high, the trailer couldn't be seen at all from the secondary road. Once the corn had been picked, a hedge of overgrown bay bushes hid where she slept.

Leeta jiggled a square of newsprint.

"Did you see this ad?"

"At the speed you're jiggling, I can't see it now."

"Okay, smarty pants. I'll be brief. Sales and gobs of them. At the mall. Jackson City. Get dressed."

"Sales on what?"

"Bunches of stuff."

"Bunches of what *kinds* of stuff?"

"Shoes, clothes, pocketbooks, sundresses, the works."

She hadn't stepped aside; Leeta squeezed into the trailer sideways.

"Hurry up!" Leeta harangued. "We're on a mission."

"A mission," she repeated, still without moving. "And who is supposed to benefit from this mission?"

"Beth! You need a sundress."

"Says?"

"Me."

She closed her eyes but that was a mistake. Once back from George and Leeta's, she hadn't stopped drinking.

Leeta jiggled her elbow with the same ferocity she'd jiggled the newspaper ad.

"Stop that!"

"I'll stop when you start. Go! Get ready!"

"Sundresses, Leeta? Where would I wear a sundress? In an air-conditioned bank? I'd freeze to death."

"Who said anything about work? This is for fun stuff. Movies, picnics…"

"Me, in a sundress, at a picnic."

"Why not? You'd look cute."

"Did you forget the game? We don't have time for shopping."

"Do so. George is meeting us at the ballpark. I've got my game shorts in the car. We'll throw yours in too. But for now"—Leeta eyed her as if deciding how to dress a doll or mannequin—"put on something brighter."

"Says the woman dressed entirely in orange."

Orange sleeveless blouse, orange slacks. Orange barrettes in red hair. No matter what she dragged from the closet to wear, next to Leeta, in the car, in the mall, she'd look about as radiant as a paper bag.

"Make tracks," Leeta said, relentless. "Jesus wants you for a sunbeam. In a sundress."

Maybe because she was still a little drunk, maybe not, the sunbeam remark set off a slideshow. Beach church with cockeyed steeple. Sandblasted parking lot. A smaller version of herself walking toward the vestibule hand in hand with Aunt Grace, recognizably Aunt Grace only before, until, a riotous Spirit overtook and transformed Aunt Grace Grim into Aunt Grace Elated.

"What's with the poor-me look? I've come to liberate you from this crappy trailer!"

But she didn't want to be liberated. She liked her crappy trailer. She'd be fine with never leaving her trailer. Ever. Again.

At various times, in high school and since, Beth had been Leeta's "fashion project." There was, for instance, the year Leeta insisted she have her lank and limp brown hair cut "spiky style…you know, like Rod Stewart."

For the five minutes it took Beth to pay for what she hadn't wanted, her head looked like a rooster's. Out in the air that "do" spontaneously drooped and flattened. Then her hair looked as if someone blindfolded had gone at it with scissors. Not very sharp scissors.

"No way!" Leeta denied. "It looks great!"

George had been home, in the shed, when they pulled up in the Mustang. Wiping down a wrench, he'd wandered their way.

To him, she said: "Thanks for not dropping the wrench along with your jaw." To Leeta, she said: "I told you. Hideous."

"No, no," protested George, ever the diplomat. "Just different. Definitely different."

"Shut UP, George! It looks terrific!"

At the absurdity of Leeta's insistence, she had finally, finally, laughed. Cautiously George joined in.

"You have my sincerest condolences, Lizzie Beth. Next time, don't let wifey use you as a guinea pig."

"It's not a crime to try something new!" Leeta sniped. "It's not noble to never change a fucking thing."

A dig—at George.

She and Leeta squabbled over hair, clothes, TV shows—nothing that truly mattered. But fighting George, Leeta sometimes went after what made George, George. And when that happened, George took himself elsewhere: to another room, to the shed, farther.

"Go after him. Apologize," she'd say.

And Leeta would say: "For fucking what? Telling the truth? About this house? This land? This life?"

And she'd say: "You love George. He's your husband."

And Leeta would say: "And what would you know about husbands, Beth? Got one stashed somewhere I don't know about?"

Inside the mall tunnel, Leeta snapped her fingers and kept snapping them.

"Perk up! Shopping with you is like shopping with a zombie!"

The mall wasn't crowded; the water fountain echoed. To no effect, she continued to moan and groan and drag her feet.

Inside the Jewel Box, Leeta ogled one after another sparkly thing. On command, she provided the wrists and neck for Leeta to "test out" the dangle of bracelets and necklaces.

Then they made a Coke-and-donut pit stop.

Then they wandered through the shoe store, sundresses still on the horizon.

Next stop, while Leeta plucked through a pile of lingerie, she slumped against a shelf of pocketbooks.

Predictably, Leeta zeroed in on red.

"Underwire. What do you think?" Leeta asked. "Is it me or is it me?"

"It's you."

"Here's one in turquoise for you."

"And whose boobs will I borrow to fill it?"

"A turquoise bra in your size, I mean. Take a look."

"Looking, not liking."

"Beth!"

Saved by an approaching salesclerk.

Or nearly.

Leeta waved off the store rep. "We know what we want."

Unfortunately what Leeta now wanted was to check out every sundress in stock. To pass the time, she spied on the rebuffed salesclerk, returned to the cash register. Leaning her hip against the counter, the clerk finger-pressed her spine.

Much was required of salesclerks. Cheerfulness, optimism—*unbounded* cheer and optimism, starting with "hello" and cycling through the dressing room peep show. A salesclerk had to be at the ready with substitutions of size and style and color. Had to pretend, handing in alternate merchandise, not to notice or be appalled by the warts, scars, thunder thighs, saddle breeches and spider veins exposed by fluorescence. Facing defects and ruin, salesclerks had to behave as if each customer possessed perfect flesh, ideal proportions. Every damaged body a pleasure to behold and outfit.

She would make a lousy, lousy salesclerk.

"Found one!"

"Bright purple. My favorite."

"Just try it on," Leeta insisted.

She stepped inside the dressing room cubicle, closed the curtain, hung the dress on the hook and started counting. At thirty, she reached over and rustled the material—what material there was to rustle. Constantly after her to "show more skin," Leeta had, no surprise, picked out a sundress that started low and finished high.

Compared to Leeta, short and compact as a kid, still short and compact, she looked over-stretched, gangly. Short hems exposed her bony knees.

"Your knees are not, repeat NOT, bony!" Leeta claimed.

"Like the Body Beautiful knows anything about bony knees."

"Look again, friend," Leeta argued, pointing at herself. "Flat feet, Dracula teeth."

"Oh yeah, Leeta. You're a real creep show."

"And so what if you do have bony knees? Hundreds of guys are addicted to bony knees. Thousands."

"Right," she said.

"It's not individual parts, it's the package that counts. Dress up the package and there you are: in the money."

Leeta swiped at the curtain.

"How does it look? Let me see!"

"In a minute," she stalled, examining a violet bruise on the underside of her wrist, tender to the touch. She remembered banging her shoulder on the doorframe at George and Leeta's. Nothing after that. Had she fallen later, getting on or off the couch? Sacrificed her wrist to spare her nose?

"Five seconds and I'm coming in."

"Cool it, Leeta."

She moved closer to the mirror, pinched the bruise, counting on pain to reactivate the memory.

The curtain flew open.

"You didn't let me see!"

"Waste of time."

"Are you *sure*?"

"I'm telling you: not my style."

Leeta backed out of the dressing room, held the sundress at arm's length, re-inspected.

"Maybe you're right. Kinda loose around the middle. More maternity dress than sundress."

She hadn't made the maternity connection; if she had, the resemblance wouldn't have counted against the purchase.

"Game time," she said.

"You only tried on one dress!"

"One dress is my limit."

"We're not finished shopping. Don't think for a second we are."

"Speak for yourself."

"No one likes the first dress!"

"See you in the car."

"You've got to try on more than one dress!"

"Give it up, Leeta," she said, walking.

"You're impossible!" Leeta shouted after her. "Completely impossible."

Impossible. Clumsy. Bony-kneed. And no one who needed a sundress —maternity or formfitting.

THREE

Like Mickey Waterman, Becca Denby had dropped out of high school. But she hadn't, like Mickey, quit because she'd felt bored or restless. She'd quit because she'd gotten knocked up. Until she started leaving the supper table to puke, her parents paid less attention to her than lint. A baby on board changed that. Now her "sin" had to be covered over with a marriage license.

To avoid the catastrophe of a shotgun wedding, she'd tried to eliminate the reason that compelled it, twice throwing herself down the longest, tallest flight of stairs she could find in Mawatuck County. But part of the baby in her was Denby. Denbys survived self-induced falls.

For a month and a half, almost two, she staunchly refused to name the father. Not out of pride or shame—to reduce complications. They weren't "soul mates," she and her baby-making accomplice. He wasn't even officially her boyfriend. They'd just had didn't-pull-out-in-time sex.

God's "laws" in play, her parents suddenly morphed into fulltime avengers, interrogation their new incentive to live. Every morning, every evening: *who, who, who?* When finally she gave in and supplied a name, her father sped off and collared the guy, demanding that he agree to do what she didn't want done. Under parental guard, they'd been driven to the beach, herded into the church and hastily joined in holy wedlock. In that spookily silent sanctuary, minus the usual crowd of writhing, moaning celebrants: a bride and groom with nothing to celebrate.

By mouthing "I do," she'd overridden the bastard status of her child without simultaneously guaranteeing him a long-term daddy. Before the seasons changed, her hubby of record skipped out. She didn't blame him. Who wanted to be a parent at sixteen? Mothers were strapped to fetuses; fathers carried a lighter load. Situations reversed, she'd have bolted too.

As a very young mother, for various pay, all of it low, she'd waitressed, clerked and sold macramé to craft shops, handing over those meager profits to her mother who ritually accused her of trying to make nothing. "You think this house runs on air."

She thought nothing of the sort. Income and independence were her dual obsessions. But until she signed up for a ten-buck correspondence course in bookkeeping, she hadn't realized numbers were her talent and her passion. Keeping ledgers, tallying up revenues and expenses, shifting funds from one column to the next made her cream.

The afternoon her box of cereal knocked against Mickey Waterman's can of Vienna sausage on the checkout counter of the 7-11, she instantly recognized him; she hadn't expected him to recognize her.

"Rebecca Denby, right? That cereal for you or the kid?"

"Both I guess," she said, feeling foolish.

As she dug for change, the cashier expressed condolences to Mickey.

"Sorry about your father, hon."

"Are you?" The Hon replied. "That makes one."

At his elbow, she giggled guiltily, amazed and frankly a little envious of anyone who so openly despised a parent, dead or alive. In the parking lot, he asked what she'd been up to besides kid care. She mentioned the bookkeeping course, nothing else to report.

"So you're a bookkeeper."

"Sort of."

"Looking for a job?"

"With a baby and no money? Nah," she said and the sullen, surly hood with a rash of chin acne laughed.

"Then I'll keep you in mind," he said, springing into a blue '62 Corvair laced with welding stripes.

"Do that!" she called after him, hardly knowing why. He hadn't seemed particularly sincere.

Six months later, still in his leather and pompadour stage, he showed up at her parents' door, causing the dog to growl and her kid to scream. She didn't invite him in; to avoid her mother's eavesdropping she walked him to the corner of the yard.

"My old man's estate is about to be settled," he announced.

"That's good," she said to be polite. What had that to do with her?

"So whatever your current boss is paying, I'll double."

"You're offering me a job?"

"What's the problem? You don't want to quit the one you've got?"

A novice at deal making back then, she'd admitted there was no other job.

"Then you can start right away. But I gotta warn you: you'll be working in the back room of the market, so expect your office to smell a little high."

"I don't care what it smells like. I'll work anywhere and I'll start today."

"Tomorrow's soon enough."

"But I'm ready now."

"Be ready tomorrow."

He waved to her mother's nose, stuck between Venetian blinds. In the Corvair, reverse engaged, he gave her parents' house the once-over.

"I see you live in a shit hole too."

Coming from another mouth, that observation might have irked her, but she knew where Mickey lived, what he lived in, despite his daddy's money. And he had said *too*. "I see you live in a shit hole *too*."

"All my life," she said.

"Times are about to change," promised the leather-clad prophet who drove a souped-up Corvair.

"They have changed," she gushed, causing his eyes to flash.

"I'm talking big league overhaul, not pissant stuff."

Since she'd irritated him already, she didn't censor. She told the bald-faced truth.

"I'm all for big league overhauls."

He'd looked her hard in the face then, as if trying to decide whether or not he could believe that response.

He could. Then, later. Trust her, rely on her, expect her loyalty and get it. Because no one else had given two-strikes Becca Denby the chance to prove she was better than her DNA suggested, no one. She owed Mickey. She'd always owe him. Whatever happened—anything that happened, anytime, any place—she had his back. *That* he could count on.

Mickey started her on a salary—not an hourly wage—with health and dental benefits for herself and her son. For as long as the roadside market existed, he also insisted Becca cart home all the cantaloupes, peaches and pecans she wanted, gratis. To justify his investment, she did more than keep books. If three customers waited in line, she scurried over to help Myra Waterman bag and weigh produce.

Three—that was the figure she'd worked out in her head beforehand as the deciding factor. Not so small a number that she'd offend Myra by lending a hand too soon. Not so large a number that Myra could accuse her of being "too uppity" to bag melons.

"Why the fuck do you care what Mama thinks?" Mickey quizzed. "You don't work for her. You work for me."

After that reprimand she did pay less attention to the woman who wore faded housedresses and between customers stood with her arms crossed, staring glumly across the highway. Marginally less. Myra was still a Waterman—she a Denby.

His mother out of earshot, Mickey didn't hide his intentions regarding the roadside market.

"When she goes, this place goes with her. Even when it turns a profit, the margin sucks."

Profit was profit, the bookkeeper in her had argued. Nothing to sniff at.

"Break your back for an extra thousand to blow at Christmas?" Mickey railed. "Maybe some other fuck. Not me."

At first, she'd biked to work. Not too taxing a trip if the highway crew had passed through and mown the shoulders, but whether the grass was high or low, she got to her job on time. The morning she heard squealing brakes behind her, she took a header into the ditch to avoid getting thrown through a windshield. Smart leap for her, disastrous for her bike. The plunge bashed the rear fender, twisted both pedals, bent the handlebars and broke several wheel spokes. Unable to ride the bike in that condition, she'd walked it the rest of the way. The kickstand also useless, she'd left her ride lying on its side behind the market—out of everyone's way, she thought—and headed to the restroom to attempt some repairs on herself. The restroom window was broken, halfway open. Yanking thorns from her hair, she heard an ominous crunch, followed by a slammed car door, and the beginnings of a major tantrum.

"Sorry, sorry, sorry," she'd bleated, running toward her twice-trashed bike, pinned beneath the Corvair's wheel.

"Piece of shit bicycle!" Mickey yelled, fisting air before he noticed her. "What the fuck??? You're bleeding."

Not much. Besides which, her boss's fury took precedence—or did until she realized Mickey was less pissed about running over the bike than about the bike itself, the fact of it—a conclusion that pissed *her* off. She'd apologize for where she dumped the bike, but she would *not* apologize for biking to work.

"I ride what I can afford, okay?"

"Definitely not okay."

The next morning, when she arrived on foot, he presented her with the keys to a pale green Volkswagen Beetle.

"Forget the dents. The engine's ready to rip," Mickey said.

"You mean I can drive it?" she'd asked, flabbergasted.

"Drive it, sleep in it, but do me a favor: don't run it into a ditch."

For the tax write-off, she'd suggested painting "Waterman Produce" on the doors and across the hood.

"You're serious? We can save money doing that?"

"Save it, make it," she said and he planted his feet, rocked back on his bowlegs, laughed.

"Swear to God, I fucking love this racket."

As far as loving each other, she and Mickey had always seen eye to eye. Respect, sure. Satisfying sex, absolutely. But love, that binding pledge to "play nice"? If she'd learned anything, she'd learned playing nice got you nowhere. Between her and Mickey, there'd be no love nonsense, no nice.

At first they'd screwed in the office behind the market that smelled of rotting produce. Once Mickey ventured into the real estate business, they "upgraded" to a motel on a backwater canal that smelled of fish and fishermen. The afternoon Mickey closed on the tract destined to become Oak Park Colony, they'd checked into the Causeway Motel to drink champagne, screw, and commemorate screwing Ronnie Ancell. Ronnie Ancell would never have knowingly sold his farm to a twenty-year-old, to a Waterman, or to any buyer who intended to break up those acres into home sites. Mickey's age, name and purpose—any of those factors—

might have sunk the deal. By hiring a discreet third party to negotiate the transaction—her idea—Mickey had pulled off a coup.

In the Causeway Motel, after putting a match to the breakdown sheet of Ancell farm profits, Mickey tossed that burn into a bathtub ringed with fish scales.

"Only fools invest in weather," he said.

She couldn't have agreed more.

Even growing up the anemic daughter of illiterate flatlanders, she'd never envied the sons and daughters of farmers. Farmers' kids looked as threadbare as herself.

In appreciation for her help on the Ancell deal, Mickey retrospectively doubled her salary, threw in a bonus and bought her a new Thunderbird—the first of many salary hikes and hefty bonuses.

Whatever storms blew through Mawatuck, her son would never be a Mawatuck have-not. Thanks to Mickey, she'd never be one again. For that weatherproof security, Mickey got better than her love. He got her vigilance.

"Sleep in once every great while, Becca," Mickey suggested. "Even our enemies go off the clock now and then."

An argument, if ever she'd heard one, to work twenty-four hours a day—most especially while the competition snoozed.

She lived ten minutes from the office, fewer than ten when she didn't have to share the road with beach traffic or combines. True, she could have lingered over breakfast with her son or extended her tub soak, but she preferred to be the first in the office and the last to leave. Unless Mickey was sleeping off a Ward Street foray on his office couch, she got her wish. On those mornings she didn't get her wish, she did what was necessary to keep boss and staff apart. As a sales force, Waterman employees were supremely competent—she made sure of that—but, regarding their "relationship" with the boss, they could be laughably naive. They worked for a bracingly blunt man. Constantly it fell to her to point out the obvious: if manners mattered more than a fat paycheck, by all means, quit and go work for a mollycoddler. Who with a brain or breath of ambition would prefer option two?

Near the front entrance of Waterman Enterprises this morning she spotted a crack in the flagstone. That flaw would have to be eliminated—today. If she noticed the crack, so might potential buyers.

Defective walkways didn't work to Waterman advantage.

Placed in charge of landscaping and architectural decisions for the office, she'd settled on a flagstone path lined with pink geraniums and an entrance porch threaded with lavender wisteria. Interior ceiling rafters, fireplace mantels and reception benches incorporated beams "saved" from old, local, falling down barns.

The soft sell of pastel followed by the sentiment of history.

"What next?" Mickey had smirked. "Mawatuck wheelbarrows under glass?"

"If wheelbarrows help close a deal, you bet," she'd answered.

A gallery of wheelbarrows, if need be.

On her instructions, the sales staff pimped Mawatuck history (a British colony before an American colony, a Carolina colony before a Carolina county), the beauty of dogwoods and the recreational thrills of catching bass. No references to chiggers, gnats, ticks, poison ivy and July's annual plague of yellow flies. Sales staff who wanted to remain Waterman reps learned to sniff out buyer bias. Accordingly, accents fluctuated from Southern to generic, political beliefs veered from liberal to reactionary, conversations progressed by means of folksy patter or a clipped, trimmed rendition of facts and figures. Whichever tactic/ stereotype hastened the sale, the sales staff obliged and enacted.

Not up to the playacting?

Find another job.

"Becca's boot camp for real estate agents," Mickey called it.

But it worked. Two years into the business, Waterman Enterprises sold seventy-five percent of all homes and land sold or resold countywide, a percentage that continued to edge upward.

As owner, Mickey received half of every commission. Sitting on his thumbs, he'd still earn ten times the amount the average Mawatuck family of four survived on. Making money wasn't the problem. The problem was Mickey sitting on his thumbs. In the absence of business adversaries, he looked elsewhere for competitors, usually in the vicinity of Bartock's Ward Street.

With Sheriff Titus Morris in their pocket she wasn't overly concerned about any incident that occurred on Mawatuck County soil. But Bartock wasn't Mawatuck. If Mickey ran afoul of the law on Ward Street, she wasn't confident she'd be able to hush up the fallout—and she liked to feel confident. Mickey had his racing; control was her rush of choice.

She flipped a series of light switches, adjusted the air conditioner's thermostat, tidied a stack of real estate brochures that had taken a skid. She checked up on the cleaning service: bathrooms, trashcans, window blinds. And then she turned her attention to the campaign. An oversized county map had replaced two mallard paintings on her office wall. Red stickpins marked the candidate's appearances; blue stickpins tracked volunteer activity. Volunteer Group Five, she noticed, was falling behind on literature distribution and door-to-door canvassing. That poor performance couldn't continue. Between now and the election, no Mawatuck voter must be allowed to forget Mickey Waterman, his candidacy or his campaign—whether or not that blitz represented the candidate's idea of a good time.

Definitely a challenge, convincing Mickey to run for commissioner, but pitching the idea, she'd pitched prepared. The Board of Commissioners' meetings were open to the public; as a Mawatuck citizen she was able to sit in on the proceedings and size up the competition. Pinched-lip Iris Forbes had a habit of voting "no"—a potential difficulty but not much of one. The sanctimonious thought highest of themselves. Focused flattery would neutralize Iris Forbes. The other four on the five-person board came off as weary men who wanted to be elsewhere, and one of them would be as soon as Mickey got elected.

For background research, she'd camped out in the courthouse archives, read and reread the minutes of past board meetings, county regulation documents and the latest development plan, supposedly compiled by an "outside consultant."

If she'd ghosted it herself, that development plan couldn't have read more pro Waterman—and, by extension, supportive of a Waterman candidacy. According to the report, Mawatuck would "inevitably" become a bedroom community of urban Bartock, "necessitating development in denser modules." Mickey was the only real estate developer in Mawatuck building residential communities, dense or otherwise.

"We should, at the beginning of this inevitable growth process, attempt to maximize the benefits of growth" concluded the development report—a ringing endorsement for Maximizer Mickey, homegrown business visionary. In advance of the population surge, Waterman Enterprises could build a state-of-the-art fire station for the county, fund facility upgrades to the public schools and "graciously" underwrite a few other handpicked, conspicuously philanthropic projects. Spill a little money here, a little money there and slowly but surely dilute the distrust associated with the Waterman family name.

Her game plan—and a good one. She'd done her homework, collected the information she needed to broach the subject with Mickey. But to improve her chances of success, she waited until he was bored enough to listen.

That hour came in January, the third morning in a row she found him sleeping off a hangover in his office. After shouldering him into the shower, she brewed a carafe of vilely strong coffee and opened the closed blinds. Rejoining her, he reclosed the blinds but accepted a cup of coffee.

"What, Becca? What are you after? You're not hanging around to enjoy my charming company."

"Promise you'll keep an open mind."

"Christ," he said, rubbing his temples.

"You've got money, land, a certain toehold on power…"

"More than a toehold," he corrected.

"But right now that power is limited to what money can buy."

He smirked at that, dumped the coffee, replaced it with scotch.

"Which makes it unlimited power. Cold cash buys all," he reminded.

"Okay. But why buy what you can legislate for free?"

"In case you haven't noticed, Becca, I'm not in the mood for conversations about nothing."

"Not nothing, something. I'm suggesting an expansion. Into politics. Run for the Board of Commissioners."

"Christ," he said again. "When did you come up with this lamebrain scheme?"

"It may not be the most important job in the world, but it's the most important in the county."

"Shared importance."

"We have to get you elected to the board before you can take over as chairman."

"You've given this more than a passing thought."

A delaying tactic, that skirt. But it also meant he was paying attention.

"I have. You can easily outspend any opponent without depleting your reserves. Win or lose, the tax advantages of a campaign are substantial. And you won't lose."

He leaned back farther in his chair.

"But county commissioner? So fucking podunk."

"You could run as an Independent," she hammered on. "An Independent can compete in the general election without competing in the primary. Let the rest of the contenders spend time and money knocking each other out. The primary winner will assume he's got it made because that's always been the case—before. While he's kicking back, enjoying his summer vacation, we'll steamroll."

Mickey opened a pack of cigarettes, pushed back, settled his boot heels on the desk blotter. She took a cigarette for herself, smoked while Mickey mulled.

If he thought he'd convinced himself, all would go easier.

Much easier.

"We'd have to set some ground rules."

"Like?"

"Like the campaign is pure sideline. Business comes first—no question, no contest. As soon as your little experiment starts to interfere, it's over."

"Of course," she agreed.

"You'll run the campaign?"

"I'd like to."

"But no tricks, Becca. You don't get to change tactics, midway through."

"Wouldn't dream of it, boss."

"Fuck if that's so," he said.

A comment she'd let pass, uncontested. No need to quibble over the finer points. She'd gotten what she wanted, gained his tacit approval to proceed and for five months had proceeded.

This morning she made a note to call and chew out the field coordinator of Volunteer Group Five. Next she listened to her voice messages. Next she checked the week's confirmed appointments and penciled in the possibility of others on her calendar. Next she counted campaign posters, calculating when and where to distribute the remainder of the stack. The usual morning routine until she glanced out a back window toward the rear parking lot and saw Mickey's Alfa Romeo sitting cockeyed, filmed in grit, left headlight smashed, front grille dented.

Which meant: forget routine. She, they, had a problem this morning —and likely multiple problems.

Candidate Mickey had spent last night dirt-road drag racing.

Candidate Mickey was bored.

"Get out, Becca."

"Late night?"

Mickey didn't bother to answer. The couch beneath his ass felt like a washboard.

"Why the fuck can't we buy a comfortable couch?"

"I wasn't aware that it was uncomfortable."

He sat up.

"When we're screwing, we're not sleeping. Or trying to."

"What kind of new couch would you like? Divan? Loveseat? Sectional?"

"Leave while I'm still smiling."

"You're not smiling," Becca said.

"Oh but I am. Deep inside."

"Now who's being funny?"

"Neither of us. Just go," he said.

She went nowhere.

"You'll get around to showering and shaving in, say, the next half hour?"

"Mothering your own kid's not enough anymore? This is you, extending your range?"

"This is me protecting your investment and my livelihood."

For some reason, for no reason, Becca's unflappable matter-of-factness enraged him this morning. His teeth had started to click and clack like a cat tracking jays.

"Afraid stubble and whiskey breath will scare off ninnies before they sign on the dotted line? I'll jack off at the front door if I feel like it."

During that spew, Becca methodically spread papers across his desk. Deposited two files, tucked another under her arm.

"It's my fucking real estate office, my fucking name on the stationery. Every other leap year try to remember that fucking fact."

"Believe me," she said, scanning his calendar, flipping pages back and forth. "You and the fucking facts never escape my attention. Which means I've noticed you've developed a case of the itchies. Why don't I arrange a few impromptu campaign appearances to keep us both entertained?"

"One more fucking word about your fucking campaign…"

"Your campaign."

"Yours, Becca. Start to finish. Your brainstorm, your agenda. So go. Play politics. Leave me out of it."

He closed his eyes, kept them shut. Maybe he'd get around to changing shirts and shaving. Maybe he wouldn't. Becca's wish wasn't his commander in chief.

"So yes on the added campaign appearances?"

"If I say yes, will you leave me in peace?"

"I'll leave," she said. "The peace part is up to you."

Fucking Becca.

Always had to get in the last word.

Last night, like every night lately, Mickey had gotten laughed at, pitied. Called an ancient, a fag, a burnt-out hood.

"Take your business elsewhere, Grandpa."

"Try me once, shitheads," he dared. "Then we'll see who's laughing."

The race he'd finally negotiated he could have won driving blind. The new ones, the young ones, drove like they had bits in their mouths, slowing for curves, clinging to the steering wheel, pumping the clutch, applying the brakes of cars supplied by Mom and Pop. Gutless wonders, all talk, no nerve, afraid to risk a popsicle, much less their necks. None of them half as hungry and desperate to win as he'd been at sixteen.

A fucking genius at scavenging junk parts, he could weld, he could solder, he could put together an engine that purred, but he couldn't mold rubber. To race the Corvair, he'd needed tires. Good tires, not patched. Blowouts got your killed. The only money he'd ever asked his father for was tire money.

"You want money? Make it," Senior said.

Stealing seemed easier than counterfeiting.

For the heist of an all-night market off Ward Street, he'd impersonated a demented vet wearing gear from the local Army-Navy surplus. Coaled his face, wore sunglasses and a pith helmet, made sure the camouflage pants were big enough to also camouflage his bowlegs. To those basics, he'd added shoulder pads, a pillow to round out his gut, hoping to pass for wider, older. For protection and to threaten, he'd carried a blade.

It hadn't been a mistake, the vet getup. Common sight: military guys going berserk up and down Ward Street. But an uncommon disguise would have worked in his favor just as well. The white middle class didn't patronize Ward Street establishments. Any clerk held up by a milk-face wearing khakis and a windbreaker wouldn't have retained the specifics. Prosperous Crackers blended together, man. They all looked the fucking same.

He hadn't bothered to search out the wimpiest cashier or the dimmest lit cash register, too pumped to put up with delays or caution. Lurching into the first late-night market he came across, he demanded the contents of the money drawer. The clerk who complied had a greasy mustache, fingers kinked from arthritis.

Sixty years old and working the night shift.

In sympathy for that poor fucked bastard he'd almost turned around and lurched elsewhere. Almost. Sympathy wasted, in any case. Tough as beef jerky, that dried up clerk. Handed over the bills the way he probably handed over slurpees—without concern, without interest. Didn't look twice at the lump of pocket thrust his way. Didn't care whether the material covered a gun or blade, fake or real. Just fucking didn't care.

Afterwards, in an alleyway, he torched the vet duds, cold creamed his face and, back in leatherwear, took in an uninspired, uninspiring striptease show, his heart flipping and fluttering from other cause. Ignore a woman and she'll wear herself out trying to get your attention. Up close he could see the stripper's varicose veins, a red slash running across the inside of her wrist. When she bent her puckered rack over him, he stuffed two twenties down her fraying g-string. He could afford to be generous. The money in his pants wasn't his.

With new tires and an engine upgrade, the Corvair was ready to compete and so was he, burning for the chance. At sixteen, seventeen, racing was the dream, his only dream. To move so fast you had to smell the route, take curves on faith.

Last night on Ward Street, he'd offered a shitload of cash, then doubled it, before he got any of those preening boys off the sidewalk and into their cars.

Last night, the cockiest of that fair-haired tribe had leaned into the Alfa, face close enough to punch.

"Okay, Gramps, you asked for it. But realize, you'll get no favors from us, no slack for age. You'll be clenching your ass every inch of the way."

Last night, like a hundred nights before, he'd answered: "Just drive. Just get in your fucking car and drive."

Sometimes he gave his wet-behind-the-ears competitors a mile. Sometimes, too far ahead too soon, he took his foot off the gas and screamed out the window, furious with those wormy fucks and their prick-timid brand of racing, more furious with himself for calling out amateurs, sinking to the level of chicken-shit city boys who wouldn't race for real, for blood.

None of them had faced a crack-up at one hundred plus. None of them had seen a buddy fishtail and flip.

"Hell yes, I was alone," Benny Luton lied to the cops when they came sniffing around his hospital bed. "Black night, slick road, end of story."

Paralyzed from the waist down, and still Benny had had the decency to cover for his fellow racers all those years ago.

A crew of Benny challengers had met up on Swampside Road, marked off a starting line. Along with everyone else that moonless night, Mickey had hoped to make racing king Benny and his muscled-up Cutlass suck exhaust fumes. And it almost happened, had been happening. Along the short, straight stretch, there'd been less than a yard's distance between the front fenders of Mickey's Corvair and Benny's Cutlass. But when they banked into the first curve, Benny misjudged the angle. To keep from slamming into the Corvair, Benny pulled too far right, lost traction. In the rearview mirror, Mickey watched Cutlass headlights leapfrog, one over the other over the other. He saw it still, that light show. He'd see it if he lived long enough to die toothless in a pond of his own urine, tubes down his throat, needles in his veins.

They'd called the cops. Had to. Cops, paramedics. There was too much twisted metal. They couldn't get Benny out themselves.

Instead of screaming, Benny had panted. Mickey wouldn't forget that either, the sound of wounded panting.

But Luton was tough, stayed tough, in a wrecked Cutlass, in a hospital bed, goosing nurses, cracking wise.

"Guess I'll be using my pinkie to press the accelerator from now on. Ain't no big thing. I got myself one strong-ass pinkie."

The cops didn't believe Benny but couldn't prove he was lying. To catch other racing liars, they set up patrols up and down Swampside. Six months after the accident, anyone who wanted to race still had to make do with rutted side roads or roads in another county altogether. An inconvenience—but that wasn't Benny's fault. Benny had done his best. Benny hadn't squealed in pain and he hadn't squealed to the cops.

First hospital visit, Mickey had brought along an Indianapolis 500 t-shirt and his entire stock of racing mags—the only payback he could afford at the time. Mickey Senior had to croak before he could set up a trust fund for the Luton brats. Waterman Enterprises had to exist before he could hire Benny's wife, Sheila, to park her neglected ass on one of his sales chairs.

And starting a company? Not immediately on his to-do list once Senior's cash was his cash. He'd had other priorities. Why invest what could be spent?

Scamming his mother out of her rights had taken two seconds, tops. Trained to keep her nose to herself, the widow signed whatever papers he plunked in front of her, no questions asked. For that helpful indifference, he refrained from dynamiting the roadside market she piddled around in. What more did he owe the relative who'd never once taken his side or come to his defense? According to his book of grievance, absolutely fucking nothing.

First shopping spree, he bought two Corvettes, a flashy El Dorado and a high-end pool table. Then a fleet of ramped up go-carts and the ongoing favors of as many whores as he had energy for. With every purchase he imagined Senior clawing to stop that money gush, but getting nowhere, man, grave dirt heavier than a deadweight corpse.

Then he got bored. With the partying, with spending as revenge. Started scouting for a different kind of playtime. It didn't take a whiz to see where the real money could be made in Mawatuck County, 1973. Staring anyone and everyone in the face. Obvious as snot. It wasn't growing cantaloupes. It wasn't growing peaches. It wasn't growing corn or wheat or soybeans. It wasn't farming of any sort. It was farmland, there for the developing.

Made me an offer on acres wet enough to grow paddy rice. You think I won't take his cash? I ain't that charitable a man. Wouldn't ole Mickey Senior throw a conniption fit? I said to Lurleen, I said: Lurleen. Don't you go running off your mouth about Mickey Junior buying swampland. Half of Mawatuck will be knocking at his door before we can sell him the rest of ours.

Whether or not the property was officially for sale, he approached owners, made offers. Every acre of cleared or wooded land that could be bought next to the river, an inlet, a creek, he bought. Bought and sold and tripled Senior's fortune and kept tripling it. Buried his shriveled mother done in by a heart as faulty as her fat husband's ticker, money pouring in like rain, like a fucking river tide.

Senior's seed money?

In comparison?

Piggybank change.

No one, *no one*, could say he hadn't made his own haul.

But so what? What was he supposed to do *now*? Rejoice that he was a bored rich guy instead of a bored beggar? Bored was bored. Then, now, every fucking minute of every fucking day.

A fistful of aspirin sliding down his throat, he walked to the back window, raised the blinds.

Becca had been busy.

In the time it had taken him to lift his ass off the sofa, the Alfa had been hauled off for repairs and the Mercedes driven over by one of her toadies. Even if he got a Ward Street punk to follow him to Swampside, in a heavy-ass Mercedes he'd never best one hundred on the curve that ended Benny's racing days and ruined his sex life.

As Becca well knew.

Fucking Becca.

Eight steps ahead as usual.

FOUR

League requirements weren't stringent—the reason Beth had slipped through.

If you were over eighteen, signed up, then showed up at the ballpark in Jackson City for practice on Saturdays and games on Sundays, you could play summer softball. You didn't have to be a talented pitcher, catcher, hitter, base stealer or supremely coordinated. You didn't need to know the rules.

A bunch of dregs and dorks in Leeta's description.

"How can anyone win with dregs and dorks?"

Since winning wasn't an outcome Beth expected, failing to win didn't count as a disappointment. Playing weekend softball in June and July was just something to do as a prelude to group drinking at Graff's.

While Leeta parked—sloppily—behind the dugout, she scanned the field. George was warming up his pitching arm, throwing to Sandy Walker. A fence separated the parking area from the playing field. Through mesh, because of mesh, both guys seemed to be covered with Xs—*X-ed out*, she thought and wished she hadn't. The idea of an X-ed out George made her anxious.

Leeta climbed across the gear shift into the backseat to change into a pair of what she called her "snuggies"—shorts that didn't bag, bunch or otherwise get in her way while running bases.

"That flappy mess you're wearing? I'd feel like I was wearing a diaper," Leeta said.

"Better baggy than crotch-splitting."

"Crotch-splitting? These shorts? Not even close," Leeta argued.

She could keep the argument going, but why? She was tired of debating clothes. Back at the mall, she'd met and surpassed her clothes-talk quota for the month.

Required to serve as Leeta's mirror holder, she tilted the compact.

"Will you keep still?!?"

"Will you hurry up? Everybody's waiting."

"Oh, so now *you're* in a hurry," Leeta observed. "I say make 'em wait. It's not like they've got better things to do."

"We're here to play ball. Remember?"

"All right, all right!"

"Those red lips gonna help you hit?" Sandy Walker jawed from first base as Leeta sashayed toward the plate.

Twice Leeta swung and missed. Then her line drive bounced past Sandy into right field.

Once on base, Leeta cupped her mouth. "Hey, boys! Did ya hear? Sandy's gonna borrow my lipstick. To improve his game."

Behind her, Sandy raised his glove. "Fire it, George. Make the Mrs. jump back."

Because Leeta was already straying from the bag.

Given a choice between hitting a homer and stealing base, Leeta would opt for base stealing. Every time.

On the pitcher's mound, elaborately nonchalant, George scratched his neck, adjusted his cap. Then he snapped the ball straight and hard toward Sandy's glove.

"Not quite," Leeta sassed, safe by a hair.

Next up, Beth dusted her hands, raised the bat, attempted to ignore the distraction of Leeta's show-off footwork. To appear minimally competent, she had to concentrate fully on the pitch and the ball coming at her—not that focusing greatly helped. She always swung too early if she swung at all.

During practice, as a kindness, George lobbed slow balls at her. But she despised that delicate handling. Despised it.

"You think Duke Cartwright's gonna go easy on me? Come on, George. You know the strategy. Practice rough."

A flash of red, an easy mark. This attempt, Leeta got tapped nowhere near second base.

George doffed his cap, bowed to whistles and applause.

"Mr. Great Shakes," Leeta jeered. "Mr. Look At Me Now."

"Well darlin'," George drawled. "That's what you get for telegraphing your every move."

"Is it? Is that what I get?" Leeta argued.

"You do."

"So says George. The expert."

"Guess who lives in the shithouse now?" Sandy informed the outfield.

"Will you guys save some for the game? When we need it?" Beth keened.

58

"I'll have plenty for the game, just like I've got plenty now," Leeta said before rushing the mound, clipping George behind the knees and hoisting.

George reached behind them both, pinched Leeta's ass and got dropped.

"Big deal," Sandy said. "A flea could lift George."

"A flea? You calling me a flea, Walker?"

Leeta advanced. Sandy backtracked.

Beth knew protest was useless but whined at Leeta anyway.

"Come on, Leeta! Get in the game."

"This isn't a game. This is practice," Leeta said. "And Walker thinks I need practice picking up lard asses."

"Hey now. Don't go hurting yourself," Sandy got out before Leeta slammed her chest into his ribs and lifted.

Suspended in air, Sandy looked with alarm toward the grounded George. To get free of Leeta, the first baseman would have to fight those tits. And because George said nothing, looked nothing, Beth said on his behalf: "Freaking out your teammates. Good plan, Leeta."

Sandy's feet returned to dirt.

"Nobody's freaked out," Leeta declared. "We're just getting warmed up. Right, Walker?"

"You're warm," George said in his usual George voice.

But the next pitch he threw was a fast-breaking curve ball. Flying past Beth, it sounded like someone sucking breath.

At Graff's Tavern, the team passed on the vacant booths and shoved three tables together. As a start they ordered three pitchers of Pabst Blue Ribbon. Cheap beer, but beer.

"Empty glass anyone?" Beth yelled down the length of the table. "Speak up! I'm pouring."

Leeta's bare leg was draped across George's knee. Absently he stroked it.

They're okay, Beth told herself. *They're okay*.

In Sandy Walker's considered opinion, Culpepper's lacked a solid hitter.

"Good outfield, though," George countered.

"The hell you say. They got nuthin', man."

"A nuthin' that catches every fly ball you hit," Leeta said and George winked.

Beginning to feel pleasantly high, Beth congratulated herself on successfully evading a sundress buy. Plus, they'd had a good practice. George and Leeta were back in sync. Tomorrow their team would challenge Culpepper's and afterwards, win or lose, they'd all come back here for another beer share.

Mellow, off-guard, lifting the pitcher to pour herself another glass, she heard violins and the beginnings of a Brothers Gibb warble. Because "To Love Somebody" was one of her favorites, she was smiling when she glanced toward the jukebox. And then she wasn't.

"What the fuck?" Leeta yelled, rearing back from beer slosh.

If there had been a lock on the restroom door, she would have locked it. But there wasn't. To keep something between herself and Leeta, Leeta's curiosity, Leeta's meddling, she grabbed and held the wobbly knob.

Regardless, Leeta kept twisting.

"Beth? Beth! You in there?"

If Leeta kept shouting, others would arrive to shout with her. And if shouting got them nowhere, there was always the option of busting down the door.

So she let go of the doorknob.

Why prolong the inevitable? She always gave up before Leeta did.

"I thought the door was stuck."

"No you didn't."

"Okay, I didn't," Leeta conceded. "But I still want to know what's going on."

"What do you think? People have to pee."

"And some people have to pee in a big crashing hurry."

"Yeah. So?"

"So after you peed, you barricaded the door," Leeta said. "What am I missing here?"

"Your beer?"

"Hmm," Leeta said, swerving toward the cracked mirror above the cracked sink to check herself out. "This story of yours? Not buying it."

To do something, she hip-knocked Leeta away from the sink and rinsed her fingers.

Leeta fluffed the bangs on her own head, then went after the stringier strands nearby.

"Quit that!"

"Why? Your bangs could use some plumping too."

"I mean it, Leeta. Keep your hands to yourself."

"Are you feeling sick? Because you look a little funny."

"So do you. In this light."

Undeterred, Leeta leaned closer.

"Will you stop with the inspection?"

"Why are you being so touchy? Can't I be concerned for your, I don't know, welfare?"

"I'm not touchy, I'm…tired. It's been a long week."

"Tell me about it," Leeta said, diverted at last. "If I had a dime for every time I yawned at that receptionist desk…"

"So can we go home now?"

"Might as well. Nothing exciting happening in here or out there."

"Grab my billfold."

"Why can't you grab your own billfold?"

"Do you have to argue about everything?"

"Okay, okay," Leeta said. "I'll get your billfold."

"I'll meet you out back."

"Out back? Why out back?"

"Because that's where I'll be."

"You are sick, aren't you?"

"I'm not sick!"

"Then why are you acting so fucking weird?"

"Because I'm fucking weird! Okay? Fucking weird Beth."

"Jesus," Leeta said, backing away. "Whatever ails you, it better not be catching."

By quarter to four, Sunday, the full team had arrived and crammed into the humid dugout. Everyone except George chewed Juicy Fruit and everyone, George included, cased the rivals' dugout.

The Culpepper team wore new blue and white jerseys.

"Snazzy," Leeta said. "We must be the only team in the league without uniforms."

"Technically, a jersey is only half a uniform," George said.

But he too seemed a little envious, Beth noticed—a rarity for George.

Their team wore whatever they wanted to wear. George wore jeans and a t-shirt. Leeta, a tank top and short shorts—not yesterday's short shorts, a different pair. Beth wore a t-shirt and sweats.

She'd driven herself over. Having her own car meant she could leave when she wanted to leave, no negotiation necessary. But sidestepping one standoff with Leeta didn't put her in the clear. It rarely did.

"Geez, Beth. Couldn't you find anything to wear in a *larger* size?"

She pointed to Leeta's shorts.

"I could ask you the same question."

"What is your problem?!? I can't say anything to you lately without getting my head bit off."

"Still attached, still talking."

"Uh-oh," George said, grinning. "Lizzie Beth's feeling feisty today."

"Unbelievable! They're putting Walter at shortstop!" Sandy Walker yipped.

A chorus of yips and jeers followed.

"Prehistoric, man."

"And knock-kneed."

"Maybe they'll leave him in the whole game."

"Check it out. Dot Jenkins at second."

"A woman?"

"A woman who'll make you look like a spaz before this day's through," Leeta warned Carl Barco.

Near the bleachers, a little girl practiced cartwheels.

The game hadn't officially begun. There was no reason Beth couldn't leave the dugout, wander over, offer pointers.

"Try *really* stretching your legs during the turn. That will help," she advised.

The cartwheeler stopped spinning.

"Know what?"

"What?"

"When I grow up, I'm gonna look just like her."

She checked to see where the finger pointed, grinned, called Leeta over.

"Don't be scared," she told the cartwheeler. "Mrs. Scaff will be happy to hear it."

"Hear what?" Leeta asked.

"When I grow up I'm going to be as pretty as you."

"You are!"

"Uh-huh, and I told my mama so too."

"Who's your mama, honey?" Leeta asked, momentarily indulgent.

"Mary Nell Holland."

"Who?" Leeta asked again, minus the grin.

Mary Nell Douglas Holland, the product of generations of Mawatuck inbreeding, the butt of "scrub her with Clorox and she'll still look dingy" jokes, the seventh of a ten-child spread, the child who'd had a child herself, age thirteen.

"A little advice, kid," Leeta said sourly. "The next time someone asks who your mama is, don't be so quick to answer."

"Know what else?" the cartwheeler asked, both of them deserted by Leeta.

"What?"

"My mama says I'm nearly grownup now."

"Oh no, not quite yet," she sputtered, afraid that if those mama words were taken to heart, the cartwheeler would be spreading legs for more than cartwheels soon—too soon. "There's no hurry. You've got plenty of time. Wait to grow up, okay?"

But the cartwheeler wasn't listening.

"Beth! Get over here!" Leeta demanded.

Sandy Walker hit a solid single that skimmed past shortstop or "the hole" as Walter's position was now dubbed. A second line drive caught Walter below the shin and bounced off. Third batter, third single. Culpepper's beady-eyed pitcher, sideburns halfway to his teeth, wiped his nose, his palms, his elbows, but unaccountably Walter wasn't wiped off the playing field.

To the competition's joy and Walter's clear misery, the hole stayed a hole.

"Re-lief, re-lief," Sandy agitated.

Next up: George.

Now the ragging came from their opponents' dugout.

"No sweat, pitcher's up."

To drown out those catcalls, Beth whistled, clapped double time, bellowed "Show 'em your stuff, Scaff!" until the crack of a solid hit eclipsed all sideline chatter.

In unison, with reverence, players on both teams looked skyward, watching the ball arc across blue, disappear briefly in the glare, reappear to drop beyond the outfield fence.

A grand slam by the pitcher! And no one more surprised than the fellow responsible. Bringing in three runs plus his own, rounding the bases, George waved his hands, shook his head, laughed.

As wife of Jock of the Moment, Leeta had dibs on first hug. To tap home plate once he got there, George had to lift Leeta off it, after which she wrapped her legs around his waist and squealed some more.

But by then all of George's teammates, male and female, were squealing—stunned, amazed, delirious, jubilant.

They were clobbering the bozos!

Because Culpepper's refused to forfeit, they played out the rout.

Bottom of the ninth, George efficiently put away batters one and two.

Beth watched from left field; Leeta semi-watched from center. They were too far ahead. Too far ahead bored Leeta.

Batter three swung. One clean strike and counting.

"Give it up," Sandy Walker pestered. "You're history, man."

"Batter, batter, batter," Beth crooned as George wound up and let loose.

The batter got a piece of the ball, just a piece.

Strike two.

A pack of folks, not players, not fans, streaked across the outfield, carrying something between them.

"What the hell?" Leeta blurted, turning, staring.

George kept pitching.

A pop-up fly, more than a pop-up, began its descent toward Leeta's territory.

"Ball! Ball!" Beth yelled while Leeta, glove down, continued to track the invaders.

Which meant Beth had to cover Leeta's position, rush toward center field, attempt to outrun a fast dropping ball, make one final, desperate, last-second lunge, glove extended—and thereafter accept the punishments of gravity.

George reached her lump in the grass first.

"Got it," she said, lifting the ball, wincing.

"Can you move your elbow?" George asked. "Do you hurt anywhere else?"

"Of course she hurts!" Leeta yelled, shoving in. "Beth, for godsake! This is softball, not football!"

"I'm good," she kept saying. "I'm good."

"Mic-Key! Mic-Key! Mic-Key!"

Leeta swiveled.

Even from ground level, Beth could see the banner. Unfurled and attached to the outfield fence, it covered three grain ads.

"Am I crazy?" Leeta asked George. "Or does that say 'Mickey Waterman, Mawatuck Commissioner'?"

George joined Leeta in the staring. "That's what it says," he grimly confirmed.

Her teammates' distraction allowed someone other than a teammate to edge closer, close in.

"Careful, Beth, careful," Matt Spruill softly urged. "Here. Take my hand. I'll help you up."

In her silent trailer, when Matt Spruill phoned, she heard at most his every third word. And one in three was too many.

Using her good arm, she levered herself onto her knees.

"Wait. Lean on me, lean on me."

Soft requests, but insistent.

When they were growing up, it was Leeta who was crazy for boys, Leeta who dated every male in three counties. Spared Leeta's constant reminders, Beth probably would have overlooked the sexual division altogether. Boys had never been a draw. But because Leeta was her best friend, because Leeta wanted her to be nuts for boys too, she'd invented Gerald.

"Gerald, Gerald, Gerald, Gerald," Leeta chanted, jumping up and down on the bed, excited by a fiction. "Tell me everything about him. Start from the beginning and don't leave *anything* out."

She'd made it up as she went along. He'd come to a family reunion. A cousin had introduced them. But she and Gerald weren't directly related. And he didn't live in Mawatuck.

"Too bad," Leeta mewed. "Where does he live?"

"In the mountains," she supplied—because there were none of those nearby.

"Wow. That is far. What does he look like?"

Blue eyes, wavy hair. Caught up in her own invention, she revealed the startling news that he shaved.

"You're lying!"

To extricate herself, she lied again.

"He also drives."

Leeta was as crazy for cars as she was for boys and demanded a description of Gerald's "wheels," fins to dashboard. But lying about cars was easy. Cars she could sound enthusiastic about.

"What else?"

"He's a lifeguard."

Too late she realized she shouldn't have said "lifeguard." Leeta wasn't a moron.

"A lifeguard in the mountains?"

"At the community pool."

Close call. Too close.

"Hmm," Leeta said, momentarily silenced, but far from finished with Gerald.

To sustain the myth that Gerald lived, breathed and considered her his sweetie, she'd been forced to generate a history, updates, love letters whose envelopes she conveniently lost before Leeta could scrutinize the postmarks. After considerable searching, she found a photo of a guy with blue eyes and wavy hair in a dime-store picture frame and coated that image with clear nail polish to improve its photographic sheen. Eventually she documented Gerald's existence so thoroughly, talked so long and so intimately about "my boyfriend," she, herself, half believed he was real.

When Leeta lost interest in Gerald, when there was no longer a compelling reason to keep a "Gerald" at the forefront of her consciousness either as a topic of conversation or as a boyfriend shield, she discovered she missed her imaginary beau. She'd developed a ludicrous affection for...nothing. And yet her attachment persisted. Part of her twenty-second birthday had been spent imagining Gerald at twenty-two and assessing his "evolution." At twenty-two, he hadn't become as tall as his thirteen-year-old height had predicted. The little scar above his eyebrow, caused by a diving mishap, had faded. Without that prominent scar, he seemed a much more ordinary, less fearless sort.

All in all, she had to admit that Gerald the fiction hadn't aged as captivatingly as he might have.

But whose fault was that if not Gerald's creator?

George wouldn't hear of Beth driving herself with a bum arm and Leeta refused to drive either the Plymouth or the Mustang directly to the trailer. First, Leeta declared, everyone was going to Graff's. George would drive the Mustang; Leeta would drive the Plymouth. And the nice fellow who'd helped the injured owner of the Plymouth ease into its passenger seat would follow.

"We'll meet you there," Leeta ordered Matt Spruill.

Matt Spruill, military man, followed orders nicely.

By appearing at Beth's side and service in left field, Matt Spruill had shifted Leeta's attention from a political banner onto himself. Now fully fixated on Matt Spruill, Leeta suddenly remembered having seen him "some place before."

Yeah.

Last night.

At Graff's.

Standing beside the jukebox.

"So what gives?" Leeta pried, once Matt Spruill had trotted off to his car. "You can tell me now or I'll get it out of him at Graff's. Your choice."

Not a choice. A threat. An ultimatum, Leeta style. The longer Beth held out, the longer it would be before they got to Graff's and beer. She and her throbbing elbow really, really needed beer. How little could she reveal and still get them moving toward beer?

"He's from Mawatuck, used to live here, before he joined the military."

"Then he's home on leave?"

"I guess. Can we go now? Please?" She pointed to her banged up elbow to gain sympathy.

"Did you know he was home? Before last night? When he showed up at Graff's?"

"No," she said—the truth for a change.

"And you met him when?"

"Grammar school."

Back to lying.

70

Actually, she preferred lying.

"Our elementary school? You're positive?" Leeta grilled. "Because I can't believe I wouldn't remember him. Was he...?"

"Younger," she said to speed up the inquisition.

Leeta's brow puckered.

"But he went off to military school before high school, right? Because I'd definitely remember him from high school. Even if he was younger. Or...wait. Unless he looks way different. Has he majorly cuted up since then?"

"You're asking me?"

"You don't think he's a cutie?"

"Not particularly."

Her elbow hurt. Her hip hurt. She wanted out of the car. She so wanted a drink.

Leeta smacked the steering wheel. "You clever thing, you! I get it! Since he's already smitten, you're playing it cool."

"I'm not playing anything."

Softball included. The team would have to find another left fielder. One who could raise her arm. One who didn't limp.

Outside of Graff's, while Leeta "did a quick hair fix," she held her elbow and peered inside, dreading what she'd see and seeing it: Matt and George, seated side by side, Matt Spruill talking earnestly, George politely listening. To what?

The Army sucks.

As a kid, did you trap that ditch beside the hog farm?

Will you please, please, please put in a good word for me with Beth?

Without expression, George listened. When Matt Spruill talked earnestly to her, she assumed she looked like a treed cat. Because that was how she felt. Cornered, no escape.

"Sure, he's a little stiff," Leeta declared, joining her at the window. "But he's still in the military. Once he gets out, lets that hair grow a bit... I mean, he won't stay in the Army forever, right?"

If only Matt Spruill *would* stay forever in the Army.

Or somewhere, *anywhere*, other than Mawatuck.

This time, when Leeta reached to fluff bangs that weren't hers, those grabby fingers got pinched.

"Elizabeth Jane Anderson! This guy is a catch! And I know for a fact you like those square-jawed types."

"Then you must also know—for a *fact*—that anyone twenty-six years old can arrange her own dates."

71

"Yeah, well," Leeta said. "Sometimes you're a tad slow on the uptake."

"And many times, Leeta Jean, you're a tad fast."

Leeta opened the door.

"You're just nervous. That'll pass."

"I'm not nervous! I'm pissed that you're hounding me to death!"

Loud. Way, way too loud.

George's head shot up, as did Matt Spruill's. And then Matt Spruill stood, smiled and came at her.

FIVE

George loved farming, couldn't remember a time when he hadn't. His own legs too short to reach the John Deere's clutch, he rode perched between the V of his father's legs. On his tenth birthday, he got what he'd long wished for: a solo ride. Jangly with excitement birthday morning, he'd run all the way to the field, started the tractor, steered toward the first row and promptly horrified himself. His maiden plowing expedition had been a travesty. Instead of working the field, he'd mauled it, wheels riding the slope again and again.

Half an acre of that and his father, from the path, gestured for him to stop.

Climbing off the tractor, shamefaced, he'd expected to be rebuked. Should have been, in his opinion: a farmer's son who couldn't plow straight.

"You think you learned now?" his father asked.

Like a sinner he'd slouched while his father spat tobacco juice.

"Need another acre to practice?"

"Yes sir. Seems like I do."

And then his ear caught the beginnings of a laugh.

"It's not funny, Dad."

He'd wanted, he'd always wanted, to disk every row of every acre beautifully, to plow like a master craftsman.

"You'll get the hang of it eventually, or you won't."

Meant as encouragement, that gruffness, but it hadn't encouraged him then and seventeen years later his initial incompetence still caused a pang. Whatever his gene pool, he wasn't a natural-born farmer. To learn how to farm right, he'd had to practice. A lot.

Practice opportunities weren't easy to come by the summer he was ten or any summer thereafter. Crops already planted, fertilized and cultivated; corn and soybeans too high for a tractor's company; any attempts to improve the year's yield long past. To while away the time, he could mow hedgerows and access paths, but those were sideline activities. Those didn't put him where he wanted to be: smack in the middle of field, nothing between him and sky except the cap on his head.

July through August, his father performed moisture checks before breakfast, always starting with the acre farthest from the house and finishing up with the cut alongside the kitchen. By then, he'd also be awake, watching from the back steps in his pajama bottoms, crunching Cheerios. Ira Scaff's sampling routine never varied. Select a spot between rows. Squat. Dig for a dirt clod. Lift it. Sniff it. Pinch it. A good sign, gummy grit. It meant the soil beneath topsoil hadn't yet been sucked dry. But rarely had he borne witness to his father's gummy thumb. Mostly he saw dirt clods turn to powder, fall and dust Ira Scaff's brogans.

Finished with farming chores for the day, his father hung up his cap, took a seat at the kitchen table and tucked into a stack of syrup-heavy pancakes. Didn't hurry through breakfast, didn't hurry doing anything. The problem was too much time, not too little. To keep himself occupied between moisture checks, his father fished the creek or holed up at Kiley's with his cronies discussing tractor mechanics, Farm Bureau reports, so and so's risky decision to plant an acre of peanuts. Allowed to tag along, little George Scaff, farmer-in-training, lunched on canned sardines, balanced his butt on bags of dog food and tried his utmost to look, sound and behave like the genuine article. By example, if not blood inheritance, he ought to have learned to tolerate summer's shutdown, endure the idle months till harvest. But there wasn't much of a Kiley's crowd to hang with anymore, and the farmers who did still gather preferred to talk about their failing health. He couldn't spend a full day on the creek casting for speckled perch. He didn't enjoy being on water. Land was what he loved.

"Right," Leeta scoffed. "Dirt, the romance."

"True love," he confirmed.

"Uh-huh. I better not catch you trying to ball a dirt clod."

"Okay, I'll make sure you don't catch me."

"Stop! Now you're just being creepy."

Not creepy—flip, because he'd long since given up trying to explain to Leeta his attachment to dirt.

"Interested in a cash-poor, dead-end profession? Sign up for farming," she mocked.

They weren't flush, no argument there. He'd inherited a 110-acre farm. The best farmer in Mawatuck couldn't get rich off 110 acres. He'd make more money commuting five days a week to a Bartock assembly line. But punching a time clock? Spending the rest of his working days, maybe the rest of his life, hunched beneath a factory ceiling?

"No one dies from hunching," Leeta said.

But from heartbreak?

As Cracker-ignorant and backwoods-hokey as it sounded, forced to give up farming, he believed he'd die of something very much like a grieving heart. If he admitted as much to Leeta, she'd assume he'd gone soft in the head. His father would have said: "We all die of something, George."

He knew that's what Ira Scaff alive would have said because that's what Ira Scaff dead said all through the long, idle summer.

Before his father died, old-looking rather than old, George had accompanied him on a tour of the property's sheds.

"I wish I could promise these tools, this equipment, will bring you luck," Ira Scaff said, tossing aside a rusted horseshoe. "But they won't."

Done with the sheds, his father continued on to the corner of the yard and George had followed, expected to follow. Together they'd gazed at the fields, his father spitting blood instead of tobacco juice. He'd stayed silent, expected to stay silent, until his father elected to speak again.

With a red knuckle Ira Scaff pointed at sprouting soybeans, pale green nubs straining toward sunlight.

"All this land you think is so...grand? When you need to sell it, sell it."

"What? No!" George had screeched, in no way prepared for that decree. "You never sold out. I won't sell out either."

Again his father spat. "Sell out. That some kind of hippie talk?"

"No, I just meant...you kept the farm. Even when corn prices dropped. Even after the hurricane..."

"Because nobody offered to take it off my hands."

"You say that now, but that's just...now."

When you're dying. Because you're dying, George thought, frantic to excuse his father's lapse in judgment and resolve.

"This notion you've got about farming being something more than putting food on your table, something holy. You've got to get that out of your head."

Never, he thought. *Never*.

"Listen to your daddy while he's still around to be listened to. You can't live the life I lived, the kind your granddaddy lived. Those times are gone, George. And they ain't coming back."

His father was tired and ill. The tired and ill were pessimistic. Maybe he couldn't live, farm, the very same as his father and grandfather, but that didn't justify rejecting the farming life altogether. The present didn't have to repeat precisely the past to honor it.

While his father coughed and dozed on the tree swing, lit upon by katydids, crawled across by beetles, he'd made a project of reorganizing the sheds. Sort, clean, tidy, preserve. By replacing grimy light bulbs with fluorescent strips, he'd been able to find and rescue what mounds of bolts, screws, pipes, hammers, belts, blades, bailing wire and inner tubes had concealed. An anvil belonging to his Granddaddy Scaff. A cypress tool chest, scored with the letters S-C-A-F-F. A mule's plow harness. A leather tool punch. Indian arrowheads of granite, quartz and mica, collected from the fields, handheld proof that people came and went while land remained.

How could he consent to be the Scaff who walked away?

How could he bear it?

It was already hot, a hot Monday's introduction to the hot week ahead. Cooler, beneath the shed's overhang, so he re-oiled the anvil, rearranged the arrowheads. He'd tuned the combine, changed the spark plugs on the Jeep, swept out the sheds, burned the trash and fixed the leaky water heater last week.

He could mow the yard.

He could do that today.

A few rangy weeds had shot up among the crabgrass. Sharpening the mower's blades, tightening gaskets and topping off the gas tank used up another few minutes of daylight.

He started mowing in the backyard because there, when he glanced up, he saw fields. Mowing the front yard, he saw cars. By next summer, he'd be mowing beside cars that whizzed by four abreast. State funds had already been allocated, the widening of 178 scheduled to begin the week after Labor Day. In theory, an improvement. A four-lane highway meant Mawatuck residents wouldn't be stuck in their driveways May through August, waiting for a hole in tourist traffic. Four lanes also guaranteed that tractors and combines wouldn't create bottlenecks during field-to-field transfers, September and March.

But he'd take inconvenience over property reduction any day.

"If your family had thought ahead at all," Leeta complained, "they wouldn't have built so close to the highway in the first place."

But how far ahead were Scaffs supposed to plan? Highway 178 didn't even exist when the house was built.

"Not that it matters anyway," Leeta grouched. "Headlights already blaze through our bedroom windows."

"Eight feet is eight feet," he said, sounding even to himself like a land nut, a land fanatic.

But that's what he was.

Finished with the back, front and side yards, he kept pushing the mower, down the field path, toward the Scaff graveyard. Mowing between gravestones was part of his responsibilities, part of his circuit, but even to fill a vacant summer's day he dreaded opening that iron gate. As loud a racket as the lawnmower made, it was never loud enough to silence exasperated ancestors.

Here he comes again, Ira. That son of yourn.

The one thinks farming's better than Christmas.

The one thinks it's fine to be money-poor since he's land-rich.

Didn't you explain to him, Ira? Didn't you set him straight? We didn't have land, we had dirt. In our hair, in our eyes, between our teeth. We had drought and hurricanes, hungry deer and sucking beetles, nature working against us, God Almighty too.

Throughout that singsongy chorus, he kept pushing, head down.

Tell him, Ira. Tell that son of yourn what's in store.

Done told him, his father said. *Ain't nothing more I can do.*

Except to repeat and repeat and repeat that *done told him* as grass flew like dust.

Driving up, Beth saw George mowing the Scaff graveyard. From a distance, because sweat had darkened the back of his t-shirt, it looked as if some black creature had taken roost between his shoulder blades.

To catch his attention, she climbed on top of the Plymouth's hood, waved the six-pack.

"Work break!"

"Hey you. Friday already?"

"Close enough," she said.

Loping toward her, he grinned.

"No argument from this quarter."

When did she ever get an argument from George—about beer, about anything? George wasn't the arguer in the family.

They settled together on the tree swing.

"The more you drink, the less I'll stink," he said, blades of grass sticking to his chin and neck.

But he didn't stink, not really. And she had plenty of drinking excuses; she didn't need another.

"Leeta running late?"

"Seems to be."

A spurt of talk, then in companionable silence they drank, mosquito hawks buzzing past.

Seven years ago this September, flecked with corn dust instead of grass, George had shown up on her trailer steps and then too, for a little while, they'd sat, drinking in silence, staring at fields—Celus Snowden's half-picked corn crop on that occasion.

At the time she'd been out of Aunt Grace's house and living on her own for less than a month.

Her choice of rentals mystified Leeta—not George.

"I can understand wanting to escape wacky Grace," Leeta allowed. "But a trailer? In a cornfield?"

"Heads up, buttercup," George defended. "Not everyone hates looking at corn stalks."

"Heads up, farmer boy," Leeta shot back. "A lot of people do."

But Beth wasn't one of those people. A trailer in a cornfield was where she lived and where she wanted to live. What else was there to say?

The day George visited solo, she hadn't realized there was anything special about his dropping by, assumed he was just taking a break from picking corn. She'd turned down the stereo but left the door open, so they could still hear Jim Morrison pleading for a lit fire. They were halfway through the second six-pack when George got around to saying what he'd come to say.

"Something I need your opinion on, Lizzie Beth."

"Okay. One opinion. No charge."

"Be straight with me now. Don't set up a pal."

"Okay," she said again, utterly clueless as to what was on his mind. "Straight talk, no set-ups."

"If I ask Leeta to marry me, do you think she'll say yes?"

She'd dropped her beer, pinched her own cheeks before cupping his.

"Oh, George, this is so great. So, so, so great. You're really going to propose?"

For George and Leeta to have married anytime would have been a thrill, but then, just then, the news seemed to guarantee two of their three the happy ending she'd wanted for all of them.

"Thinking about it, Lizzie Beth. Considering it hard. But not if you advise against it."

"But I don't advise against it! Ask her!"

"Because you're sure she'll say yes?"

"Surer than sure. But wait—this calls for something stronger than beer!"

And so they'd whiskey toasted and toasted and toasted George Elias Scaff's decision to ask Leeta Jean Porter to be his bride.

"I want to marry her. I do."

"And will."

"Will I?"

"Yes! And it's going to be fantastic. Do you know how fantastic it's going to be?"

"I'm gonna ask her," he said. "I am."

"When?"

"Soon."

"Tonight, George! Drive straight from here to Leeta's house. Do it!"

"But if I do, and she turns me down, I'm gonna blame you, Lizzie Beth," he said, drunker than she was.

To hear the proposal details, Beth had to wait for Leeta to get drunk.

"Did he get down on one knee?"

"Are you kidding me?" Leeta said. "He practically walked in on his knees."

"And he took your hand?"

"Actually, he took hold of my ankle."

"Leeta! Cut it out. The truth now. He popped the big question and you said…"

"Why not."

"You said why not??? To a marriage proposal???"

"What's wrong with why not?"

She'd groaned, feeling the way the proposer must have felt at that response.

"Stop groaning!" Leeta berated. "I agreed, didn't I? You and George! Wanting some big declaration of together forever. What the fuck do I know about what will or won't happen? I can't predict the future. I might get knocked in the head tomorrow and forget there is a George Scaff."

But that hadn't happened.

Thankfully that hadn't happened.

George hadn't forgotten Leeta; Leeta hadn't forgotten George. They were together, together still.

She slid across the splintery tree swing, draped an arm across his shoulder, squeezed.

"Yep. Summer," he said, mistaking her relief for commiseration, her satisfaction for dismay.

Leeta slammed shut the door of the Mustang with her ass.

"Don't take it out on the car!" Beth almost called—but neither Scaff seemed in a joshing mood.

Nearly as much as he loved the woman who drove it, George loved the Mustang. As soon as a rust spot appeared, he was on it.

Sanding off rust spots bewildered Leeta.

"I mean, why bother? It's an ancient car. With or without rust spots, it still looks like a piece of junk."

"A '65 Mustang, junk? Woman, we own a classic!" George never failed to say. "There are people who'd pay good money to own your wheels."

Leeta's comeback also never varied: "Oh yeah? Where are all these people with their good money? Bring 'em. Because I'm fucking open for business."

"Beer here!" she called.

"Give me," Leeta said.

"Shall I order pizza, ladies?"

"Sounds good," Beth answered because Leeta said nothing, taking over George's swing seat, kicking off her sandals. To distract the grumpy, Beth spread wide her arms. "See how busy your hubby's been? Not a blade of grass higher than an inch."

Smirking, Leeta pressed the beer to her throat.

"Sausage or pepperoni?" George called from the kitchen, waving the phone.

"Who cares? It's too hot to eat," Leeta said.

Leeta did look flushed. Even her ears were splotchy red.

Regardless, George persevered.

"Your vote, Lizzie Beth?"

"The works!"

The kitchen window was open. There was no cause to yell. But she wanted to sound enthusiastic in Leeta's stead. Leeta usually chose the toppings.

"If it's made in Mawatuck, it'll taste like shit, whatever's on it."

Even for a Monday, Leeta's funk was extreme.

"Bad day at work?"

"Bad work, bad drive, and something that feels more and more like a bad fucking dream."

"What's that?" she asked, despite not wanting to hear Leeta's bad dreams. She had her own bad dream stockpile. No further contributions necessary.

"Mickey Waterman running for commissioner. There's not an inch of highway between here and the hospital parking lot that isn't papered with his name."

"Going after the commuters, I guess."

"What's that you're guessing, Lizzie Beth?" George asked, rejoining them.

"That the Waterman billboards between here and Jackson City are aimed at commuters."

He'd asked, she'd told, but George seemed to have lost interest in the explanation as well as the conversation.

Unlike Leeta.

Leeta's rant was just revving up.

"And what makes Mr. Pock Face think he can get elected dogcatcher, much less commissioner?"

"They love him down at the bank," she said.

"Mickey Waterman *Junior*? Our age Mickey?"

"Our age, several lifetimes richer," she qualified.

Why did she keep contributing her two cents? Whether Mickey Waterman ran or didn't run for office made no difference to her.

"Rich from a vegetable stand?"

"Catch up, Leeta," George said. "Mickey's in the real estate business. Oak Park Colony, Oak Park Extension."

"And when did this happen?"

"It's been awhile," she said.

And then, for no reason she could fathom, George added: "Who'd have thunk? Mickey Waterman slips one by Leeta."

"I don't hear you laughing, Slim."

"No."

"And why's that?"

"Because Mickey Waterman doesn't amuse me."

"Says the man who's been known to cackle at wheat."

"Wheat is funnier."

"Funnier than Mickey electioneering? I don't think so."

"I do."

"Do you now?"

George picked up an empty beer can, tossed it at the shed. When it hit tin, it pinged.

"Which leads us back to why," Leeta said.

"And if I say why I'm not amused, you'll drop the subject?" George asked.

"We'll see," Leeta said.

"I give my opinion, end of discussion. Take it or leave it."

"Jesus crap. Get over your fucking self."

"Leeta," she interrupted.

"Pipe down, Beth. All quiet on the set. George Scaff is about to make a pronouncement."

Why *was* George acting so huffy? It was only county office. There were mailmen who held county office in their spare time.

"Okay. Here goes. My once and final explanation. I don't think Mickey Waterman running for commissioner is funny because I think it's dangerous."

Leeta hooted.

"Let me finish. He owns half the county, now he wants to run it."

"Bowlegged Mickey Waterman? Not in a million years," Leeta said.

"You asked, I told."

"Fuck you," Leeta said.

"Guys, guys," she pled. "Drink more, fight less."

Glaring, Leeta swiveled.

"Oh? Did I leave you out? Because I meant to say fuck you too, Beth. Fuck you. You should have brought me up to speed about Mickey Waterman."

Should she have? For what reason? Mickey Waterman wasn't part of their universe. He never had been.

Half asleep, Beth still recognized the M.O.: impatient, uneven blows.

Leeta, definitely Leeta, once again battering her door.

But why so early and why on a workday?

Because it *was* a workday, wasn't it? Tuesday? Yes, Tuesday. She hadn't drunk her way through an entire week. Not yet.

"FINALLY! I was beginning to wonder if you were dead in there."

"I was asleep. Like you should be."

"Not sleepy. Come on. I need you to take a ride with me."

"At dawn?"

"It's not dawn. And what if it is? You're up."

"I am now."

"Just get in the car."

"Like this?"

She was still in her day-worn/night-worn clothes. Her tongue felt mossy, gums coated. She could smell her own breath as well as her crotch. She needed to shower, brush her teeth. She didn't have time for a ride with Leeta.

"If you don't stop dithering I swear I'm going to...pop!"

"And if you don't stop screeching, I swear I'll start."

A lie.

Leeta's shrillness was as much as her brain and body could stand— and a little more besides. Had she finished the bottle before calling it a night?

On the way to somewhere, she dozed. Since Leeta was driving, she didn't really need to know where, did she?

"Wake up. We're here."

Here being the entrance gate of Oak Park Colony.

"You got me out of bed to park beside a gate?"

While Leeta stared through the windshield, she must have dozed again, memories substituted for dream. Before Oak Park was Oak Park, there'd been a road through Ancell acres that dead-ended at a river cabin visited less by duck hunters than by trespassing high schoolers such as herself. From the roof of the cabin, if you got your arm sufficiently behind it, you could lob a beer can over the reeds into the river or *on the* river, if there'd been a hard freeze. Either the can splashed and sank or clinked and rolled. Either way it disappeared.

"Can you believe this?"

She opened her eyes without replying, nothing to say. It didn't seem to strain belief, what stretched in front of them. Houses, angled between trees.

"How could Mickey Waterman have become Lord of Mawatuck and I know nothing about it?"

It *was* weird that Leeta hadn't noticed. Before billboards and banners advertised Mickey's candidacy, billboards and banners offered Oak Park lots for sale, the Waterman name prominently attached. None of the construction had been done in secret.

"Maybe because you commute in the opposite direction?"

The best excuse she could generate at this hour of the day.

"Still. George knew. You knew."

"I work at a bank. Banks deal in mortgages."

"Which you never mentioned."

She shrugged. Why would she discuss mortgage loans with Leeta? It wasn't as if either of them was in the market to buy a house.

"I need to get back," she said. "The beautification of a bank teller takes time."

Obviously a joke. But Leeta wasn't in a cut-up mood.

"Do you know what George admitted? After I woke him up in the middle of the night? After I body-blocked the fan?"

"That he was hot?"

"Five years ago, Beth—*five years ago!*—Mickey offered to buy us out."

"So what? Mickey's probably offered to buy every farm in Mawatuck."

"For two hundred thousand dollars. Two hundred thousand for three sheds, a falling-down house and wormy corn."

"*Your* falling-down house," she said.

Her stomach had begun to knot.

"Do you realize where I could go, what I could do, with that much money?"

"You and George, you mean."

For richer or poorer, she was thinking. *In sickness and in health.*

"I mean who wouldn't get the fuck out of Mawatuck, given the chance?"

She tried to picture it: life without George and Leeta, life in Mawatuck without them. Trying to keep down what was rising, she swallowed and swallowed again.

She got her head out of the car. She did manage that, clunking her chin in the process. Her puke on Oak Park pavement looked like a miniature pond, a squiggly yellow river.

"Jesus Christ!" Leeta yipped.

"Amen," she said and puked again.

SIX

Tuesday morning Becca joined Mickey and a senior broker discussing the Tillings property, a slow mover.

"Drop in on Marshall this afternoon and don't leave until he understands no one's going to pay seventy-five five for a two-stall barn and a brick four-room with no land. He's got to throw in some acres or chisel the price. One or the other," Mickey said. Then a pause. "When did we first list it, Becca?"

"Three months ago," she said.

"Too long. I want it off our hands soon."

"Should we be interested in terms of Waterman holdings?" the broker asked.

"I'd want it a lot cheaper than seventy-five five. For now concentrate on expanding the package. See how far you can push Marshall Tillings."

"Break a few legs, bust a few knuckles?" the broker joked.

Mickey faked a laugh. She recognized the fake; the broker didn't.

"Whatever it takes."

"Leave a copy of the specs on my desk, John," she said. "I'll also give it another look. We may need to slant our ads differently."

"Will do."

Once they were alone and finished with real estate business, she shifted to her campaign clipboard.

"Marion Honeycutt called. She wants to do a profile for *The Herald*."

"Marion Honeycutt. Was she yearbook editor?"

"How does Thursday sound? Before the photo op at Bevin General?"

"Either yearbook or newspaper. Owl glasses. Chewed hair."

"Then she's snazzed up since. These days Ms. Honeycutt is quite the chic lady reporter."

"But not then," Mickey stubbornly insisted.

"The point is she raves about you in her column. Now."

"Yes, but why does she rave?" he mused.

His question, not hers. Flattering quotes were the sum of her interest in Ms. Honeycutt. But she needed Mickey to sign off on the interview, move along.

"Maybe she had a crush on you."

"Maybe I raped her under the bleachers during half-time."

"Doubtful. She's much too fond of you for rape."

Then he laughed for real.

A laughing Mickey she could work with—and on. But how long would the boss's benign mood last this particular morning? Mickey lived nine-tenths infuriated. A mistyped contract, a missing signature, a leaky pen—anything could set him off. And she empathized, she did. If you're raised by a tyrant, fury accumulates. With every deal she closed, with every client she manipulated, on every occasion when one of the office staff scurried to do her bidding, she broke another bone in Buck Denby's slapping hand—so to speak. Harder to satisfy and harder to curb, Mickey's fury. Much, much harder.

"So what am I in for? Another Becca pep talk?"

"No pep talk. Schedule update. Tomorrow, we'll put in an appearance at the Ruritans' fish fry. Thursday, a sit-down with Maid Marion before the Bevin General breeze-through. Friday, Luke's King Pins."

He groaned.

"Friday is bowling league day. The place's packed with Mawatuck voters."

"You're not going to make me bowl a frame, are you?"

"If the circus pulls into town between four and five, you'll get to ride an elephant too."

"You threw that in to see if I was listening," he said. "Becca Denby, politico."

"Mickey Waterman, commissioner," she followed up.

No kicking. No screaming. Mild resistance but no absolute refusals to participate.

Good.

The less time she had to spend placating the candidate the more time she had for seducing the electorate.

For Becca's meet and greet exhibitions, Mickey drove the Mercedes. He had nothing against the car, he'd fucking bought it, but when he drove a beige car wearing a beige suit he felt like part of the beige fucking upholstery.

While Becca gave last minute instructions to her lackeys, he stayed in the car. Wherever the doctors parked, it wasn't in this lot. Beat to crap rattletraps. Pickups missing antennas. Mustangs sprouting rust. Windows smeared with brat buggers.

He'd had a kid in the Mercedes once. Becca's kid, Toby. Back when Toby was younger. Drove him to school because Becca wanted to stay put for a return call from New York.

"Which ride you up for, sport?" he'd asked prior to departure. "Smooth or speedy?"

"The Mercedes or the Alfa, he means," Becca translated.

Leaning hard against his mother's leg, dressed like a fucking prince but with the big eyes of the cautious lonely, Becca's kid.

"It doesn't matter."

"It doesn't matter, *sir*," Becca corrected.

"Either way, I'll make sure you get to jail," he'd promised.

Becca poked the clinger's shoulder. "He's kidding, Toby. Mr. Waterman is making a joke."

"Oh."

Just "oh."

A kind of breathless holding, stillness as camouflage. He remembered that dodge all too well. Who the hell ever knew what an adult meant or intended? Even with a mom like Becca who coddled instead of tormented, a kid was at the mercy of guesswork.

A tap.

Window rolled down, all he could see was Becca's self-satisfied grin. If she got any more stoked, she'd bounce like a ball.

"We'll give the crew a few more minutes to snow the lobby with leaflets," she informed him, "then we'll saunter in."

"So this is your idea of a productive day? Parking lot of a fucking hospital, lobby of a fucking hospital?"

"It is this day," she agreed, still hustling him.

"I can't believe I let you badger me into this."

"'Skillfully persuade,' I think you mean," she teased. "Besides: it'll be a kick—you'll see."

"Your kick, not mine."

"Always happy to share."

"Enough with the chirpiness, Becca. It's bringing on a migraine."

Becca wiggled her finger at him, grin intact. "No time for copouts, Candidate Waterman."

"No? Keep pushing and you'll see how fast Candidate Waterman can off his own campaign."

Blink of an eye, he thought. And if he really put his mind to it, half that.

Before they made their grand entrance, like a breeder about to show off her prize stud, Becca inspected him one final time.

"What? Not dapper enough for the polyester set?"

"Just checking, boss. Just double checking."

When the automatic doors slid open, Becca's darlings were still swarming, shoving buttons and flyers on anything with a pulse. Half the visitors in the waiting room looked like they needed a shot of oxygen. Since Becca walked in front of him, his view of the reception desk was briefly blocked. Then it wasn't.

A little fatter in the face, a little droopier in the tits. Hair still dyed. Fingernails still damp and ragged. Eye shadow creased and smeared. And now, below that eyelid blue, a dawning recognition of who he was as well.

He stopped in front of the desk, smiled. Kept smiling to show off his now perfect teeth.

From stunned and amazed to pissed and resentful to the eye blaze of who the fuck does he think he is? Leeta Porter travelled.

Apparently his pricey beige suit packed benefits beyond a flattering fit. Mickey Waterman the transformed, Leeta Porter the very same or a shade worse.

Compare, contrast, and fuck you, cunt. This ain't high school anymore.

Oh yeah. Oh yeah.

Becca was right. This was a kick. To make Leeta Porter squirm in her drawers, he'd have gladly paid the hospital an entrance fee.

Mickey had been scouting a race, not a fight, when Arnold Kaison and Billy Preston ambushed him on West End Road.

Kaison owned a blue GTO, Preston a white Impala. Coming around the curve into two sets of headlights, he'd slowed, had to. The Corvair wasn't heavy enough to ram through a GTO/Impala roadblock.

Kaison's paw of a hand appeared flat on the windshield. Preston reached inside to snag a leather lapel.

Morons—but only two, he'd thought, dragged farting into the night.

Then he saw, heard, the rest of them: an audience backed up against woods on the darker side of the road, agitating for the fun to begin.

He'd been wearing what he always wore: boots, leather jacket, pegged pants. A fake Hawaiian shirt.

What a greaser.

What a throwback.

The guy belongs in a cave.

Girly taunts. Mouthing off at him, the sideshow, while their dates fingered their snatches.

"This road's closed to dipshits," Kaison brayed, belching beer.

A single blade couldn't take them all.

"You want to get home tonight, you're gonna have to take a detour," Preston said.

Bullshit, start to finish. They weren't going to allow any fucking detours.

Wrenching free, he'd run for the Corvair, jumped in, shifted into reverse, gassed the engine, tailspun, would have escaped, except for Preston and Kaison's accomplices.

Surrounded, he didn't stand a chance. The Corvair rocked and he rocked in it, like a kid jammed in a bumper car. Julie Macmillan, Kaison's fuck, bounced onto the hood and pressed her boobs against the windshield.

"Monkey in a cage," she howled. "Monkey in a cage."

"Get off, Jules," Kaison yelled. "We're gonna flip 'er."

To save the Corvair, he'd sacrificed himself, pushing out into a wheel of fists. Determined to remember every blow, who delivered it and how, he'd succeeded in staying conscious. Kaison and Preston lost interest first. Without ringleaders, the game lacked momentum, the supporting players drifted elsewhere. He heard the GTO, the Impala, depart. When he judged it safe to move, he crawled from the ditch bank to the road, back to the Corvair. Leaning against the right front tire, hugging his ribs, he dripped blood on his Hawaiian shirt. With the eye that hadn't swelled shut, he saw her coming, the bitch who hadn't had enough of his blood and hurt. Her ankle bracelet glinted in the Corvair's headlights, toes naked in sandals.

With the arm that still worked, he threw fists of gravel at her and got the same gravel kicked back at him.

"Leeta, you coming or not?"

"In a minute, Mike," she said.

Above him, she taunted: "Hey, loser. Know what's worse than losing a fight? Being the loser no one wants to fuck."

He made a grab for her leg—to send her skidding on her ass. But she was less drunk than he was blind. Laughing, she teetered clear of his reach.

"Mickey Waterman, the hood that couldn't."

"Leeta! Get your ass over here!"

And then the bitch obeyed. The bitch obeyed.

Leeta Porter hadn't, like a conscientious employee, stayed at her post. The Bevin General receptionist joined the campaigning hubbub in the hospital's coffee shop.

Mickey chatted up coffee shop personnel, coffee shop customers, interns, orderlies, whoever wandered into that caffeine and sugar bin, always aware of the twat sulking on the stool in the corner, the twat he'd like to knock to the floor, press a boot to her throat and leave gagging.

But he restrained himself.

Why rush a good time?

Eventually he and Becca stood in front of her perch.

"Allow me to introduce…," he began—purely to fluster Leeta Porter.

"No introductions necessary," Leeta blurted.

"I'm sorry," Becca said, following his lead flawlessly. "You're…?"

"Leeta Porter, Mawatuck High School's Most Popular back when," he supplied, hoping his teeth gleamed.

"Leeta Porter *Scaff*."

"A pleasure to meet you, Mrs. Scaff."

"You're not meeting me! We were in high school together!"

But Becca had strolled on.

Maybe Becca had faked the amnesia—or maybe she truly didn't remember. Why would she, necessarily? Leeta Porter hadn't kicked gravel in her face on West End Road.

The receptionist was staring at him like a covetous beggar. Like he'd won the lottery. Like some fairy godmother had bonked him in the nads, turning him rich and successful with a magic wand. Nothing the fuck to do with him—his brains, his drive, his ambition.

Still a fan of ankle bracelets, he almost said.

Almost.

"So you grew up to hand out visitor passes at Bevin General."

"At least I'm recognizable."

"And that's a good thing?"

Just like that, he had her squirming again.

"Mickey Waterman, begging votes from a thousand and one billboards."

"So you noticed the billboards? Great."

Serenity rattled her. So he remained serene.

"What happened to the tattoos?"

That was her best attempt at putdown?

Pathetic.

She should sign up for lessons with Becca.

"Gone," he said.

"Along with the acne pits," she said.

"Isn't money amazing?"

"I wouldn't know," she said, then curled her stupid lip.

You mean you and the hubby aren't happy as turds living in that Scaff tear-down? You mean you don't prefer cheap-ass sandals?

"Mickey?"

"Be right there," he called to Becca. To the going nowhere Bevin General receptionist wage slave, he said: "Nice to catch up."

"You'll never get my vote."

He turned back.

"No? Not even if I offer to pay big bucks for it?"

"What did you say?"

"You heard me."

If he tossed his wallet on the linoleum, she'd probably dive for it, right here and now.

Dive for it. Or hump it.

When Becca ordered one of the minions to drive her Audi back to Mawatuck and hitched a ride with him, Mickey figured he hadn't looked suitably appreciative when the dumpy candy striper asked for his autograph. Hadn't adequately praised coffee that tasted like oil spill. Neglected to compliment the hospital volunteers for their "fine and selfless dedication."

Some campaign-related faux pas.

But no.

Nothing but nothing escaped Becca's attention.

"Old flame?" Becca inquired.

"Hardly."

"And was that her choice or yours?"

"You're the one who arranged the hospital visit, remember?"

"And very glad I did—on several levels."

"Meaning?"

"Leeta Scaff is married to George Scaff, right?"

"Since she insisted on being called Scaff, I'd say chances were good."

"Some divorced women keep their married names. Easy enough to check, yea or nay," Becca said.

"Why bother?"

"Because it occurs to me that we went after the wrong Scaff, trying to buy that property. However little the hubby makes off corn and soybeans, a hospital receptionist makes less. Could be the missus is gangbusters for selling."

Becca: already out of the gate.

"Well?"

"What?"

"Shall we zero in on the wife?"

"I'll consider it," he said.

"Don't consider too long."

"We don't have to own every dirt clod in the county, Becca."

"We don't?" She laughed. "Since when?"

Since the dirt clods closest to Leeta Scaff belonged to George Scaff, a nutcase about farming but still a decent guy.

"Give me a week to work on her," Becca persisted.

"A full week? Losing your touch?"

"Okay. Less."

Fucking Becca.

She'd turn anything into a challenge.

"How about five days, starting now? Come on, boss. I'll invent some bonding moment she and I shared in the halls of Mawatuck High. The 'old school chums' routine."

His turn to laugh.

"After the snub you just delivered?"

Becca shrugged. "Then I'll try something else."

"The ever-versatile Ms. Denby."

Becca smiled. "At your service. Now lemme at her."

He stopped the Mercedes at the front entrance of Waterman Enterprises, reached over her lap, opened the car door and refrained—but just—from shoving her and her clipboard onto the pavement.

Becca was in pester mode and he needed to think.

For the boots, the tattoos, but primarily for the hair, Mickey had been crowned a tough little queen in gym class.

Ooo la la.

Watch the queen preen.

Since he had no intention of playing martyr, at the onset of that locker room mouth off, he'd reached for his blade.

"No queen, but I carve real well. Come on, big dicks, try me."

As soon as the surfers and hippies and jocks found themselves on the receiving end of a point of steel, they backed off, shuffled out.

Spineless pricks.

He hadn't known anyone was behind him, so when George Scaff suddenly appeared, wrapped in a towel and knocking the water out of his ears, it had come as a surprise and not a good one. Swinging round, he swung with an upturned knife.

"Whoa, whoa," George Scaff had yelped, palms up and out. "I'm just trying to get to my clothes, man."

He hadn't exactly extended permission, but he hadn't lunged to crosshatch that hairless chest either.

Extend the farmer's tan and George Scaff could have passed as a surfer boy. He had that surfer-boy-let-it-ride vibe; he had that surfer-boy-sun-bleached hair. Near-naked, that close to a jittery hood with a blade, George Scaff must have been nervous, but he hadn't looked nervous. He'd looked supremely calm and collected, trucking over to his jeans and t-shirt, zipping up, toweling off his hair. Like a guy with nowhere to go and lots of time to get there: that's how George Scaff came off.

"Great knife, by the way. Used to have one like that myself for trapping. Sharpened good, good handle, solid blade."

"Yeah?"

"Yeah, but not nearly as nice as that one. I found mine laying around the barn somewhere. Where'd you get yours?"

He couldn't help it, stop himself. He loved talking knives. He would have talked knives with fucking lunchroom workers. He spewed forth a list of manufacturers, retailers, local outlets, blade lengths and thicknesses, the best blade for the best price and on and on.

"Blues on Ward Street will take any form of payment," he blathered. "Even a trade. I could get you a good deal at Blues. They know me there."

"Yeah?"

"Yeah."

"They keep those in stock, you think?"

"I can check, you want."

"Yeah?"

"Yeah."

"It would be cool. To have a new one. But probably expensive. Right?"

Another few minutes of chucking it up and he probably would have made a present of his own fucking knife—or promised to steal one for George Scaff.

They were the only ones left in the locker room. Even so, George Scaff checked the bathrooms, lowered his voice before saying: "You know, if Coach Casey catches you with that…"

The friendliest of warnings.

Cordiality? Directed at the five-foot-eight, 120-pound weakling who lived in black elevated boots, styled his hair in a pompadour and sported the two-in-one stench of b.o. and gasoline?

A distinctly new experience.

He appreciated the gesture, ignored the beware. Later that same week he did get caught, flashing his blade in a spot less secluded, less male. Caught—then expelled for the rest of the month.

"No skin off my back," he'd yelled over his shoulder, leaving the principal's office, tarrying in the hallway just long enough to strike a match against his boot heel and light up in a no-smoke zone.

In the Corvair, freewheeling dirt and twigs, he tore past his classroom's windows, open wide to September's breezes.

"Fuck you fucks to hell," he'd yelled, picturing all those rule followers stunned by his nerve and bravado. All those star achievers of Mawatuck High School: amazed, envious, admiring the fuck out of Mickey Waterman Junior.

In his head, that's the way it played.

Five years ago, when Mickey invited George Scaff to join him for a beer, he'd half expected to end up marooned on a bar stool, guzzling warm beer solo, fending off waitress attempts to coerce him into ordering a million-calorie pizza.

So to see George Scaff actually coming through the door of Graff's?

The afternoon's first surprise.

You could always peg a farmer, man, even in his clothes. Ankles pale as a baby's, neck and hands solar blasted, that red-brown laid in as deep as any Ward Street inking.

At the time, he, himself, had been trying out a cowboy look. Rawhide pants, rawhide vest. A tactical mistake, wearing rawhide in August. He sweated rivers while George Scaff looked entirely comfortable in his recreational flip-flops, shorts and t-shirt.

They sat on adjacent stools, a pretzel dish between them. He'd meant to ease into the topic. Instead he blurted: "My old man tried to bankrupt the rest of Mawatuck farmers, including your dad. I'm aware of that."

George Scaff had nodded once, between swigs.

"So I wouldn't blame you for not hearing me out, but I'd appreciate it if you would."

George Scaff didn't say: "Go on, I'm listening." But he kept drinking.

"These days? Farming? Losing proposition."

"Depends on how you define losing," his bar mate qualified.

"But even if you're lucky, even if you manage to keep out of debt this year, what about next?"

Leaning a little too close, selling a little too hard over a mere second beer.

"You're a smart guy, George. You see the trend. Higher seed prices, lower grain prices. Corn and soybeans that cost too much to plant, too much to pick. Only takes one out-of-commission combine to put a small farmer in hock for life." To slow himself down, he'd plucked at the rawhide sticking to his thighs. "With retirees moving in, the solid money's in real estate."

"Your business," George Scaff said.

"Yours, too, if you want it to be. You own property free and clear."

No question he was up against the badmouthing coots at Kiley's.

Common knowledge, son: a Waterman's gonna offer rock-bottom prices on prin-ci-ple. Undervalue the land. Try to make a farmer panic.

You ain't tellin' Ira's son nuthin' he don't already know, Mel-vin.

Maybe not, but best to be reminded here, among friends.

A lot those fucks knew. He'd been prepared to offer—and did—a far, far better than market price for the Scaff farm.

"You could keep a cut for yourself, build a new house, farther back from the highway and traffic."

"Think I'll stick with what I have," George Scaff said. Polite—but firm.

He'd hoped for a different response but hadn't counted on it.

"Okay. But if you change your mind, will you give me chance to beat anybody else's offer?"

"Sure," George Scaff said. "But that day's never gonna come." And then, looking down, his bar mate said: "Nice boots."

In response to that compliment, he'd also looked down, admiring his own Tony Lama footwear.

"But not as nice as those biker boots you used to have," George Scaff continued and raised his bottle.

"Fucking Christ! You remember those boots, man?"

"Sure. Silver buckles, studs."

"I loved those boots, man! Had them sewn and heeled till the repair guy refused to work on them anymore. 'Do yourself a favor,' he said. 'Throw these in the trash and buy yourself a new pair.'"

"They were great boots," George Scaff said.

"The fucking best."

And then they toasted long-gone footwear, by which time he was closing in on drunk.

"If you don't mind my asking"—and fuck him if he did—"why'd you come? You didn't care how much I offered. Your mind was already made up."

"It was. Made up, didn't change."

"Those farts at Kiley's warned you against doing business with me."

"That they did," admitted George Scaff. "But they made the mistake of prefacing that warning with: 'If he's anything like his daddy...' And I don't happen to like that judgment link."

"Sins of the fucking father," he said.

George Scaff nodded. "Sins of the fucking father."

SEVEN

The majority of Mawatuck women waited until they married to change addresses, but Beth hadn't waited for, or wanted, a husband. She'd moved out of Aunt Grace's house into the trailer because she wanted her baby to be born and raised in a home that belonged solely to her. Even on a bank teller's salary, she could afford to rent the trailer.

It rented furnished. An undersized couch, two-person dinette, Venetian blinds speckled with fly wings. A battered chest of drawers. A bed so low to the floor that when she sat on it her shoulders were closer to her knees than her knees to her ankles. Electric heat, electric stove. A refrigerator she'd planned on covering with her daughter's artwork.

She'd always assumed she carried a daughter. And if she'd carried her to term, she would have named her daughter Leeta.

After reading an article on babies and germs, she'd set about disinfecting the trailer. Although her baby wouldn't be exposed to air for months and months, she'd wanted to prepare in advance.

Balanced on a dinette chair, cleaning the upper shelves with ammonia, she felt the room tilt. Carefully, carefully, she climbed down and stretched out on the floor. In that position she came nose to nose with dust bunnies, bread crumbs black as raisins, hives of mold. But when she saw the upturned thumbtack, she immediately reached for it, its danger the most obvious of the surrounding treacheries. Thumbtack in one hand, other hand cupping her stomach, she tried to stay positive, think positive, but couldn't help herself. With each wave of queasiness she more and more feared what lay ahead: labor and its (possible) complications. If vertigo derailed her, how would she manage the pain of childbirth? Mothers were supposed to endure all grades of suffering for their children. Could she?

By the time her stomach settled and she felt steady enough to rise, she decided to postpone further cleaning. A temporary postponement, she'd thought at the time. As it happened, she'd given up cleaning permanently.

Before moving in, she bought a set of Pyrex dishes and four yellow canisters. The canisters hogged all but a thread of counter space. Preparing a meal around them was a challenge. But very soon fat canisters and skinny counters didn't matter one way or the other because she gave up cooking too. Hungry enough, she stuck her hand in the refrigerator and broke off a hunk of cheddar cheese.

For safekeeping, she stored the prematurely purchased yellow baby bonnet and sweater in the dresser's bottom drawer, further safeguarded by tissue paper.

Such plans, such ambitions she'd had!

They'd be partners, buddies. They'd share a connection that no one and no bad news could wreck. They'd survive together, help each other survive.

And then she woke in a bloody bed.

She miscarried her baby before it looked like a baby, failed as a mother before officially becoming one. She hadn't lived two weeks in the trailer before losing the reason she'd moved into it.

"All you had to do was sit back, grow fat and lazy," the tuxedo summarized from the shadows. "The most natural of assignments—and you couldn't follow through."

Against that charge, she had no defense. None. She was pathetic, incompetent. She'd been unable to protect and defend her baby's life. She deserved the abuse, God's abuse. And drunk, she accepted it.

The very first time Matt Spruill telephoned, Beth supposed he'd found her number by searching under Aunt Grace's name in the phone book—or maybe he'd simply asked his parents, who still lived in Mawatuck, for the information. Maybe his parents, eager to help, had consulted their own phone book and cheerfully relayed the seven-digit code that provided their son access to the niece of Grace Anderson. Because he'd graduated too late for a Southeast Asia tour, Matt Spruill was stationed at Fort Bragg, training recruits. From Fayetteville, Matt Spruill, anyone with a car, could reach Mawatuck in a few hours' time. Calling was even quicker.

The first time he'd called, he'd opened with: "Hi, Beth. This is Matt Spruill. I saw you at the bank the last time I was home."

She thought he'd said that. Matt Spruill murmured. Then and later, Matt Spruill and his voice sounded farther away than they actually were.

"I guess you don't remember me."

"I don't, no."

"That's okay," he said, absolving her when she hadn't asked to be absolved.

When he invited her to go to the movies the following weekend, inexperienced in the etiquette of accepting or declining dates, she committed the first of many errors by failing to say no instantly. Her hesitation he interpreted as consent.

Face to face, he seemed younger than any Army-enlisted guy should be. The severe crew cut showed every freckle on his scalp; where several freckles ran together, the cluster resembled a birthmark.

As a civilian he slouched, apologized for the weather, the traffic—nothing within his control, nothing that was his fault. During the film he bought her a box of popcorn she didn't want, also a soda. After leaving Jackson City, they rode around Mawatuck. She pointed out the new ABC store. He asked about the demolition of Bodie's Tackle. Back at Aunt Grace's house, beneath the blue-white porch light, he solemnly asked permission to kiss her goodnight. Again, she hesitated. Brushing against hers, his lips felt sticky. Her hand on the doorknob, he asked: "Do you like surf fishing?"

"I don't know," she admitted. "I've never tried it."

Hesitation and honesty—neither her lucky charm.

The next morning he showed up with ham sandwiches, Oreo cookies, bait and two of his father's stainless steel fishing rods.

Persistent, Matt Spruill.

Dedicatedly persistent.

Whatever else the Army had toughened, it wasn't skin. He'd been standing less than an hour in the surf when his nose, his cheeks, his shoulders and the backs of his knees turned a vibrant pink. He looked a little like Archie, the comic strip character.

How could anyone take seriously courtship by Archie?

Despite his fishing attempts, their only catch of the day came deep-fried and decorated with parsley, served in the restaurant attached to the pier, the restaurant's walls strung with crab netting that trapped conchs and starfish. Each time a wave crashed and pounded the pilings below, their table swayed. As the sun dropped, he ate his slice of pecan pie and hers. She ordered a third beer.

Then he suggested they adjourn to the roller rink.

Holding to the rail she inched forward, and he inched close behind. Rank amateurs among a crowd who skated hard and fast, they plodded into the whirling mass and when she fell, attempting to help, he fell also, taking her down a second time.

Something of a surprise, his klutziness.

She'd assumed Basic Training required a certain amount of coordination as well as stamina. But what did Matt Spruill's klutziness matter to her? She wasn't his girlfriend; he wasn't her boyfriend. They weren't destined to embarrass each other in public every weekend for the rest of their lives.

Done with skating, they wandered behind the rink to sit before breaking waves and stare idly at two blues, sky and ocean. Serenaded by rink music, they scrupulously avoided discussing the military, banks or banking, a vacuum that eventually got filled with commentary on nature and natural disasters. He talked about fishing, the skiff he'd built with his uncle. She talked about hurricanes.

They'd been toddlers when Diane struck, but both retained a hazy recollection of its effects. Mawatuck parents, guardians, elders in general, made a habit of loading up the family and driving to the scene of destruction. Air where there had been structure, water where there had been shore. A few years after Diane, Donna blew through, downing power lines four counties inland, ruining corn crops, killing livestock and people. When the tides of Donna receded, they left a brown waterline on the walls of Aunt Grace's church. The congregation worked for weeks cleaning out debris and still the sanctuary smelled like the bottom of the sea.

Agnes arrived in June of '72. With George and Leeta, she surveyed the splintered lumber, hollowed rooms and snarled, exposed wiring littering the shoreline. The old Coast Guard station had lost its underpinnings. After the worst of the storm had passed, for a few hours more, the structure waffled in its allegiance—would it hold to land or topple into the currents? In the end water won the contest, carrying the porch, the walls, the roof, the entire building, out to sea. Up and down the radically narrowed beach, property owners, scavengers and gawkers such as themselves walked among stranded bathtubs, mattresses weighted by kitchen sinks. Couches, toilets, washing machines, window frames— the everyday ordinary—turned topsy-turvy, dry-docked in queer configurations of ruin.

For miles she and Leeta and George had walked a beachscape of chaos and absence. The bingo hut, the carousel, a cluster of pink cottages built in the 1920s—Agnes took them all. The owners of the spared Trading Post had hung a photograph beside the cash register: a telephoto view of a gargantuan wave momentarily suspended above a cottage. It seemed impossible that a photograph could be more unnerving than the 3-D version they'd walked, but it was. The cottage was doomed. To look at the photograph was to see the end coming and stand helpless before that finality.

The ocean that stretched in front of her and Matt Spruill denied its force with a soothing wash of surf, the smallest ripple of waves, the kind of ocean that served as backdrop in romantic tearjerkers.

He asked her to smear his sunburned back with Noxema. When she finished, he detained her hand. She thought it must hurt, that burn scraped by sand, but he didn't complain. Sex was quick, awkward. Since it wasn't thrilling for her, why would it have been for him?

When she missed her period, she told no one. Aunt Grace would have been shocked and ashamed. Matt Spruill, a virtual stranger, would have insisted they marry. Leeta would have been horrified.

Even in high school, Leeta had been adamantly opposed to babies.

"Stretch marks, stretched vag, sour-smelling whiners constantly pulling on your sore tits? No thanks!"

Regardless, while she was pregnant and even after she wasn't, she chose to believe that Leeta the Second would have won over Leeta the

First. George would have loved Leeta the Second on sight and ever after. He'd have ridden her piggyback, tickled her tummy, squired her around the fields, taught her to play poker and pitch a strike. On the weekends, as a foursome, they would have barbecued burgers at sunset, counted falling stars as night drew in.

A family they would have been. George, Leeta, Little Leeta and Beth.

God wants good. He wants his followers rich and healthy. It's the Devil who wants sickness, poverty and despair. Embrace God's goodness. Hold it to your heart. If you believe with all your mind and soul in the goodness of God, He will grant you health and happiness and riches. Only lack of faith thwarts the reception of God's blessings.

Beth had spent too much of her childhood in the sandblasted church with the wobbly steeple; she had spent too much of her life living with Aunt Grace. Even if she hadn't lost the baby, she wouldn't have been able to escape the Pentecostal influence entirely, exist totally godless. So she compromised, improvised. When she slept she dreamed of her belly deflating, her fingers grabbing for something that wasn't there—so she tried not to sleep. At first the stand-in she invented seemed an improvement: amusing company during nights long and lonely. But what started out amusing didn't stay that way. With each appearance her substitute deity grew cattier, more malicious, revealed more of His nasty side. Eventually she had to cop to the obvious: her concoction didn't really break the mold. Her tuxedo God was as harsh, as judgmental and as uncompromising as the Pentecostal God He replaced.

On the plus side: the tuxedo detested Holy Rollers and matched her drink for drink.

Once He'd coalesced behind Leeta in the trailer. As always, He brought His own booze. Settling in, He'd adjusted His cufflinks, jiggled His shiny left shoe. When He started to hum, she must have blanched.

"What's wrong?" Leeta demanded. "Is it my hair? Is it sticking up? Do I need to…"

"Get her to talk God," He needled. "Go on. You know you want to."

"No," she said.

"No, it's not sticking up or no it's not my hair?"

"Would you rather I sing? *Come my love and be with me, Little Liza Jane. And I'll take good care of thee, Little Liza Jane. Ohhhh, Little Liza, Little Liza Jane…*"

To cut off the song, she'd yelled: "Leeta! How do you picture God?"

"What do you mean 'picture God'?"

"The God in your head."

"I don't have a god in my head."

"Okay, but when you think about God, what's he…like?"

Leeta frowned and kept frowning. "Why are we even talking about this?"

"Just tell me!"

"Okay, okay! Talks loud. Maybe with an echo?"

"Methodists!" the tuxedo sniffed, stirring His cocktail with His pinky. "Such feeble imaginations."

Leeta whirled around, checked behind her, whirled back. "What do you keep staring at?"

"Try again, Elizabeth," He dictated. "You can do better and so can she."

"That's what He *sounds* like. What does He *look* like?"

Leeta's God had a big head. Carried a calculator and a slide rule. Wore a baseball cap, carpenter's pants and gloves.

"What kind of gloves?"

"I don't know," Leeta moaned, fed up. "Leather?"

"Why the gloves?"

"To hide his blistered fingers, I guess?"

"You're not describing God, you're describing the devil!"

Leeta shrugged. "I kinda get them confused."

On what grounds could she legitimately protest? Her tux version was a mishmash. A little bit God, a little bit Devil.

"A little of everything, Elizabeth," as He often reminded. "Hence: God."

EIGHT

On Friday, Beth drove directly from the bank to George and Leeta's. Before leaving the Plymouth's protective custody to scoot across open yard, she scanned Highway 178, both directions.

It was officially the weekend.

Furloughs were granted on weekends.

Wiping his hands, George materialized from the shed.

"Miss Lizzie Beth! Wanna practice fly balls?"

"Me practice, you mean."

"Wouldn't argue against it."

George could almost always make her laugh. But as she laughed, she wondered: would it be wiser, safer, to park the Plymouth behind the sheds?

"Where's Leeta?"

"Inside," he said without elaboration.

"Coming in with me?"

"I'm good," he said and returned to the shed.

Joining Leeta gave her an excuse to quit the yard and she took it. But George's hanging back, refusing to make it a threesome, was…different. Suddenly uneasy for other cause, she looked again over her shoulder. But George had said: "I'm good." That's what he'd said.

"Leeta Jean? Where ya hidin' out?" she called, as if hiding were the order of the day.

No response.

The bedroom's window shades had been haphazardly closed, one pulled lower than its twin. Makeup and hairclips spilled from the dresser onto a chair piled with towels and curlers. Propping open the closet door, a shadowy heap of tank tops, shorts and nightgowns.

A foolish but cheering thought: she could hide out here. In George and Leeta's dark bedroom. Use their mess as camouflage.

"So I guess I'm not the world's worst housekeeper," she said to the bulge in the bed.

The fan spun and whirred, causing the curtains to ripple. In her bank teller uniform, she was severely overdressed. Arm slung across her eyes, covers kicked aside, Leeta lay in her underwear.

If Leeta was sick, why hadn't George said so?

"Hey," she said, less jokey, more concerned. "You okay?"

"Super," Leeta said without lifting the arm from her face, without moving anything but her lips.

"It's cooler in the living room."

"Fuck if that's so. There's not a cool spot in this fucking house."

She took a seat on the edge of the bed. Because Leeta doused herself with Ambush every morning, the smell of cologne mingled with the smell of feet.

"What's up? What's going on?"

Leeta snorted.

"Going on? Around here? A big fucking nothing as per usual."

"We can make some beer disappear. We can make that happen. I'll drag George in."

"Fuck George," Leeta said with such viciousness Beth lost a moment's breath.

"Don't say that. Please don't."

"Why can't I say 'fuck George' if I want to say 'fuck George'? Talk's still cheap, isn't it? I can still afford to fucking talk, can't I—or is that now impossible too?"

She reached over, touched the ankle bracelet.

"You're just feeling the end of the week, that's all. There's practice tomorrow, then the game. That'll help."

If offered that bromide herself, she wouldn't have felt reassured. Matt Spruill had showed up at the ballpark before. Why wouldn't he again?

"Don't try to make me feel better! Because you can't. I'm a fucking receptionist with a fucking third-hand car, living in a third-hand dump. And none of that's going to change. None of it."

But that's a good thing, she wanted to say.

She could tell Leeta about Matt Spruill. Lift Leeta's spirits, improve Leeta's mood, by confessing to the mopey what previously she'd kept to herself. Get Leeta off George's back by offering up her own.

"Case of beer says I can cheer you up."

By wagering beer she guaranteed she'd be taken seriously. Leeta sat up.

"And for this beer contribution, I'd get…"

"A secret."

"Whose?"

"Mine."

"Fat chance."

"Think so?"

Leeta turned on the bedside light, attempted a stare-down.

"You're bluffing."

"Am I?"

Leeta chewed a fingernail, deciding.

"Okay. You're on. One case of beer for one big bad secret."

"Matt Spruill doesn't want a first date. He's after a third."

Success. Leeta gaped, then popped her hard on the shoulder.

"When?"

"The first date?"

"First *and* second," Leeta demanded. "When?"

"Years ago."

"How many years?"

"Years and years."

Leeta popped her hard again. "In high school?"

"Thereabouts."

"And where did you go on these so-called dates?"

"To the movies. Fishing."

"Fishing?"

If the subject hadn't involved Matt Spruill, she'd be enjoying herself. She never took Leeta by surprise.

"So how about that beer run? Remember, you're buying."

"And here I thought you were my best friend," Leeta said with a peculiar flatness.

No longer smiling, pulse quickening, she said: "I am your best friend, Leeta. Of course I am."

"Really? Because best friends don't usually lie to best friends for years and years."

"I didn't lie. I just didn't tell every little bit of every little thing that happened to me."

"Same thing," Leeta said and turned her cheek into the pillow. "But don't worry. I'm up to speed now. You'll have your secrets and I'll have mine."

"Leeta! Come on!"

"Get your beer money from George. Tell him I said to pay."

"Stop. Don't act like this."

"Just leave, will you? You're blocking the fan."

"Leeta!"

Pleading for someone's attention who didn't want to give it.

121

In the dim corner by the closet, she thought she saw the glimmer of a pointy shoe.

The tuxedo needn't have squirreled himself away in Leeta and George's closet to make the point. She was perfectly capable of recognizing her punishment—and its justice.

Turnabout's fair play.

Kicked out of Leeta's bedroom, Beth headed back to the trailer early —too early. It was still light: outside, inside.

The phone rang.

She didn't answer.

It wasn't Leeta calling to invite her back to the house. She knew it wasn't Leeta. The soft and softer voice she'd hear if she picked up the receiver would be Matt Spruill's, "just checking in," "just saying hi," just wondering whether she'd changed her mind "about getting together real soon."

Because Matt Spruill believed if he overwhelmed her with invitations to dinner, to the beach, to the movies, she'd ultimately surrender.

And why wouldn't he believe that?

She'd surrendered before.

On those days, evenings, in those hours when she forgot, slipped up, goofed, reached for the receiver and that soft voice began its wheedling, she tried to shut it up and out with claims of conflicting plans, ill health, exhaustion...

Excuses with expiration dates.

Whereas Matt Spruill had learned from his previous mistakes, she hadn't. At the start of his second siege she should have been blunt, belligerent, obstinate, outrageously rude. Falling short of those extremes seemed only to encourage him.

Twice he'd left notes taped to the screen door along with food. A bucket of oysters. A plate of barbecue double wrapped and sealed against varmints, cooked by Ruritans at a Ruritan fundraiser.

Matt Spruill's father was a Ruritan.

Matt Spruill, husband, father, would be a card-carrying Ruritan too.

Of course he would.

She threw away the notes, threw away the oysters. Unwrapped the barbecue and left it on the steps to feed the very varmints Matt Spruill wanted to deprive. After he'd surprised her at Graff's, she threw out "To Love Somebody." She'd never again be able to listen to it without thinking of him and if he drove up and heard that particular record playing, he'd take what he heard as another sign of their compatibility: they liked the same song.

As a child, she'd liked "Jacob's Ladder," lyrics that wearied her now.

We are climbing Jacob's ladder
We are climbing Jacob's ladder
We are climbing Jacob's ladder
Soldiers of the cross.

Hard to climb, a ladder leading to heaven. To reach the first rung, any person—adult or child—would likely have to leap.

Every round goes higher, higher
Every round goes higher, higher
Every round goes higher, higher
Soldiers of the cross.

"Hymns!" the tuxedo hissed, wriggling His shoulders in revulsion. "Must we go there, Elizabeth? Must we?"

This late afternoon/early evening there were new touches to His outfit and appearance. Red socks instead of black. A red carnation in His lapel. Traces of lipstick—or so it appeared. Also a dusting of blush.

"Your gentleman caller…," He started in.

"He's not my gentleman caller," she said.

"A very *red* fellow," He continued, referring, she assumed, to Matt Spruill's hair and freckles.

Now she understood the point of His costume's red effects.

Connect the dots.

Connect the mock.

"The almost daddy of your almost child," He said.

Since He knew what she was thinking, it wasn't absolutely necessary to speak. Speaking interrupted drinking.

"There is a simple solution."

In dealing with Matt Spruill, He meant.

"Focus, Elizabeth. What has worked in previous situations? To throw others off the scent?"

Lying.

"Precisely. One of the few things you are exceptional at."

The only thing, He meant.

She wasn't opposed to lying to Matt Spruill. It wasn't a question of conscience or principles or morals or ethics. The sticking point was energy. To launch a counter-campaign of lying would require determination, discipline—Matt Spruill's strong points, not hers. How often, how vigorously, and for how long would she have to lie before the Army man gave up on her once and for all?

"What's the problem, Elizabeth?" the tuxedo jeered. "Afraid you won't be able to stay the course? Afraid, once again, you'll bungle the follow through?"

He lit another cigarette, brushed invisible lint off His sleeve. His glass on the table refilled in the manner of miracles. Hers too. She was falling into night patterns, night rhythms, falling away from what was.

And then the other red yanked her back.

A truck's approach, Matt Spruill's truck. She recognized the grind of the engine, the strategy of the driver. Matt Spruill took on the ruts of the field path with methodical consistency. Not slow, not fast, but steady. Steady on.

She was able to get away from the windows, crawl into the hallway and curl her head between her knees before the tapping started.

Matt Spruill knew she was at home.

The parked Plymouth gave her away.

The tuxedo vanished. Staving off the Army man, she was on her own.

Once, twice, Matt Spruill circled the trailer. To get closer, he bushwhacked through weeds. A thump—his forehead?—against window glass.

"Go away," she whispered. "Go away."

A second thump.

She covered her ears.

Stupid of her: to think, hope, that Matt Spruill wouldn't come and keep coming. That he wouldn't fight on, confronted with obstacles. That he'd falter in the face of adversity. That he'd give up before conquering the territory. Army men were trained to stick it out, vanquish the resistant, triumph.

And who was she? A lone woman curled up in the hallway of a tin trailer.

Easy to defeat.

He returned Saturday morning with tools. Which specific tools and how many Beth could only suppose, based on the chopping and hacking.

Prior to taking on her briars and brambles, Matt Spruill didn't knock on the door, roust her from bed. Without notification or permission he launched his campaign to restrain and tame her wild, unruly yard. Starting at the far edge, he doggedly worked his way toward the trailer—and her.

She might have crawled back into the hallway to hide again. But it was early morning. Last night she'd severely depleted her alcohol supply. What remained wouldn't get her through the day and Matt Spruill's pruning. Sooner or later she'd have to leave the trailer, go forth and deal with him, sober.

Why postpone the inevitable?

In her nightshirt, she rinsed out two stained cups and heated a pot of coffee she didn't want. It was too early to put anything in her mouth or have anything put there, most especially Matt Spruill's pink tongue.

So that he wouldn't later offer, she bundled the garbage herself and carted it to the backyard barrel for burning. He waved cheerfully as she passed, a can-do man disturbing a drowsy morning, busy with armloads of green.

When she brought out the coffee, he drank it, sweating. She still hadn't changed from the nightshirt. It wasn't a provocative gesture; she'd meant to get dressed before she made the coffee. She just hadn't managed to make good on that intent.

After he'd finished trimming the pyracantha bushes that ringed the trailer, they could "breakfast out," he suggested. In the meantime, she could shower and get dressed.

A plan.

A schedule.

She need only nod her head, fall in line, salute.

Instead she stared at the stain on the lip of her cup.

"You eat breakfast, right?"

To preempt a lecture on the nutritional importance of Meal One, she made clear her indifference to iron in the blood, calcium in the bones, enamel on the teeth.

"No doubt you'll keel over doing calisthenics at ninety," she said.

"I do hope to remain active," he answered cautiously.

"So you eat bran and live another twenty un-constipated years. It's not as if you have a true choice: life or death."

"I didn't know you felt so strongly…," he stammered.

And why would he know anything about what she felt or thought? They'd spent twelve hours together, total. He knew where she lived, where she worked, and now he knew she tolerated high grass and made dreadful coffee.

"You think by calling, coming, mowing grass, you improve your prospects? You think persistence is the ticket here?"

His smile tried for winning.

"Is being with me so awful?" he asked.

She left him sitting on the steps.

While he continued to destroy the tangled, concealing vegetation she loved, she watched from inside. When he'd finished that enterprise, she rejoined him, carrying the last of her beer stock. He took what he was handed but held the can unopened.

"Do I always start drinking before nine on Saturday?" she asked for him. "Yes. Always. Also on Sunday."

"Beth, I," he said.

She didn't want to hear any statement that began "Beth, I."

"Once, Matthew. On a beach, after roller skating, after fishing, after sunburn."

"I don't mean just the sex. That entire day we got along. We did," he insisted.

"One day," she said. "What's one day?"

"It's a start, isn't it?"

"Can't you let it be? Can't you please let it be?"

"We'd be good together, Beth. Better than good. I really believe that."

Believe, beliefs. Good, goodness.

More of what she didn't need clarified or want to hear.

She knew precisely what Matt Spruill believed in, exactly what he defined as "good": hearty, chipper togetherness; full-term, healthy babies; mowed grass; college funds.

Soldiers didn't pick apart the American Dream; they defended it, lived it, perpetuated it.

Which was where she came in: to live Americanly, Matt Spruill required a wife.

NINE

This week, on this occasion, when the entrance doors of Bevin General parted and Mickey strolled through, the receptionist wasn't at her welcome desk.

He took a moment to survey the bitch's nine-to-five lair.

Fluorescent lights, plastic chairs, chipped ashtrays, nonstop Muzak. For company, the waiting room's glazed-eyed and jittery.

This gig made bagging peaches in a market lean-to seem like a fucking holiday.

Beside the elevator, two pink-coated volunteers gossiped.

"Heard the latest about Doctor Davis? When he told the wife he wanted a new life, she said: 'Sure. You and Nurse Turkell have my blessing. All I want is the boat, the beach house, the Cadillac and half of everything you earn from now till you die.'"

"Sounds like a fair deal to me," said the other.

"My very words, sweetie."

And then they sniggered in unison.

Nurses humping doctors and vice versa—he assumed that was par for the course. He also assumed Leeta Porter had tried to stick her finger in the physician honey pot—unsuccessfully. If she'd succeeded, she wouldn't be handing out plastic passes and going home to farmer George.

He glanced again at the packed waiting room, seats at a premium—a fair indication that the beds upstairs were also full to capacity. Bevin General was doing a bang-up business. Becca should do some snooping, find out which investment conglomerate had the inside track. Waterman Enterprises might want to join in the profiteering. Grandmas keeling over in their garden daisies, witless vacationers paddling toward undertow and riptides. Someone was making a killing off death, dying and sickness.

Investment of a lifetime, man.

Leeta Porter's ass was hanging off another coffee shop stool, milkshake and mauled Twinkie close at hand. Her chum behind the counter, a block of a woman, saw him first.

"Didn't expect to see you back so soon, Mickey Junior. Must mean you haven't got the election all sewed up."

So a member of the coffee shop morning crew despised his guts. So fucking what?

For collateral advantage, he'd play along.

Smiling large and larger, he extended his hand.

"Nothing's sewn up until the votes are counted, ma'am. Are you, by chance, a Mawatuckian?"

"I am."

"Then I hope you'll consider voting for me. I'd sincerely appreciate it."

Leeta Porter sputter-laughed, sprayed.

As if noticing her for the first time, he turned.

"Leeta. Nice to see you again."

The receptionist looked worse today than she had on his last pop-in. A pimple expert, he spied two erupting near her nose, despite the slather of pancake makeup.

"Mickey Waterman, Mr. Sincerity," she said.

"Absolutely," he agreed.

"And Brylcreem free," she said, a cow with Twinkie bits on her cheek calling attention to appearances.

He plucked a paper napkin from a nearby holder, offered it, tapped his own cheek for guidance. Was mocking Leeta Porter going to be this easy? Was he never going to have to break a fucking sweat?

As if on cue, two candy stripers rushed in and squealed his name. While he milked that opportunity, Leeta Porter scrubbed at herself.

Embarrassed? Resentful?

He'd take either/or.

By following the candy stripers out, he got to the receptionist desk ahead of her, bided his time disturbing a stack of dog-eared plastic.

"Excuse me," she said, yanking out her chair. "Some of us have work to do, you know?"

"Unless they're sucking down Twinkies."

Humiliated? Furious?

Now they were rolling.

"Speaking of Twinkies, how about lunch?" he inquired.

"I've had lunch."

"Not today. Tomorrow."

"Is the candidate running low on lunch dates?"

"Not even slightly."

"Either way, I decline."

There, just then, she thought she had him. Flipped her hair, shimmied her shoulders. Smug-ed up, as if she'd just turned down a hood's invitation to the fucking prom.

Stupid cunt.

He leaned in close enough to smell her Twinkie breath, lick her clotted teeth.

"What's the matter, Leeta? Afraid you can't handle the new Mickey?"

"New Mickey, old Mickey. All the same to me."

"Prove it," he said.

"Gladly."

"Gladness won't be necessary," he said.

For their lunch "date," to out-dress him, she'd decked herself out in ruffles and bangles, wedged her feet into peep-toe high heels.

Walking toward that eyestrain, Mickey managed not to laugh or sneer. Quite the accomplishment in his estimation. Nothing short of heroic.

Crossing the Bevin General parking lot, she stumbled. Courteously, he offered assistance.

"Don't play the gentleman with me. Because we both know you're not. A gentleman."

So Leeta Porter was incapable of making a point, then shutting her trap.

Useful information.

"Not a gentleman, but a…? Fill in the blank."

"Someone who thinks he's got everyone fooled."

"But not you," he said.

"Definitely not me."

"Because Leeta Porter's too smart to be toyed with?"

"Something like that."

And then they reached the Mercedes.

"Your car?"

"One of them."

Go ahead, he wanted to say, *tongue it*. Because she looked like she wanted to swallow it whole.

She stroked the hood, the fender. Once in the passenger seat, she eyeballed the dashboard and every needle and dial on the instrument panel, squeezed the leather under her knees.

He didn't interrupt the worship. Let her fucking swoon. Unchecked envy would also help his cause.

"Nice car," she said.

"It is."

"A hell of a lot better than a junk Corvair."

A muscle in his cheek jumped.

"Roadblocking a Mercedes. How much fun would that be?" he asked.

She was still squeezing the fucking seat.

"With you in it? I'm guessing about the same."

Bitch.

She'd pay for that one.

The Cozy Corner was quiet, out of the way, pricey enough to impress a receptionist.

Mickey waited while she studied the menu.

"Decided?"

"Steak."

Because she thought steak was the most expensive entrée. It wasn't. He ordered the most expensive. Scallops, the un-priced special of the day.

A greedy eater, Leeta Porter.

He raised his hand.

The waitress brushed off the table, Leeta's side.

For dessert, he ordered coffee. Leeta ordered pie and pudding.

"Just can't seem to decide between them," she said gleefully, as if paying for two desserts would bankrupt him.

"Why not the whole dessert cart?"

"Guess you're not used to healthy appetites."

"Not as healthy as yours."

"So let's hear it," she said, shoving lemon meringue aside to get at coconut custard. "Your big campaign speech. Why I should vote for Mickey Waterman for commissioner. That's what this lunch is about, right?"

He didn't say yes; he didn't say no.

"Over the next twenty years a lot of money is going to be made in Mawatuck. As commissioner, I'd like to make sure the people pocketing it are natives."

"That covers about ninety-five percent of the population."

A cunt, okay. A cunt who ate like a sow, marginal. But an ignorant cunt who ate like a sow?

"Not even close," he said. "Not anymore."

She shrugged, scraped at the custard dish.

"As far as my qualifications for office: I'm diversified. A real estate broker, a property owner. My father was a Mawatuck farmer and businessman. And I've picked up a bit of legal know-how along the way."

"All-around Joe."

"All-around Mickey."

"So that's it?" She pretended to yawn.

He looked elsewhere. Another eyeful of Leeta Porter meal mush and he'd barf.

"You've talked. I've listened," she said, playing the queen granting an audience. "Now I need to get back to the hospital."

"Do you?" he asked, tossing cash on the table.

If she couldn't take her eyes off fifty bucks, what or who would she do for a hundred?

"I work there. Remember?"

"So quit."

"And sell Avon?"

"No. Work for me."

"Hardy har har."

Said her mouth.

The rest of her had tensed up nicely. He could hear her breathing. Little shallow breaths. Like she was sucking in her gut—or holding back a fart.

"I'd pay better than your current wages. Say your receptionist salary times three."

"Bullshit," she said.

A conversational placeholder only.

He watched her madly try to calculate the give-me value of X times three, her nit-size brain obviously bungling the job. Attempting to concentrate, Leeta Porter looked…challenged.

"I can have a contract drawn up to that effect. If you'd like to look over the paperwork first."

The disgusting fingernails plucking at the tablecloth had been chewed to the quick, but Leeta Porter did have some self-control. She hadn't yet filled her mouth with fingers.

"And if I say yes, what exactly would I be doing to earn my big salary?"

He swung his gaze higher than hands or boobs and fixed it there.

"Answering phones at the office, helping out with the campaign as necessary. Nothing too strenuous."

Funny, how desperately she wanted to take him at his word, believe it was possible, what he promised; believe that she actually could snag that big a something for that little a nothing.

If she threw in with the hood.

"Think it over. Talk to George."

"I will," she said.

Would she?

If she did, her husband would strongly advise her to keep the job she had. Because unlike his slutty, grasping wife, George Scaff had standards. The question being: would—or could—George Scaff impose those standards on his wife?

It was three in the afternoon and no bottle, capped or open, stood on Mickey's desk. More encouraging: the Mercedes was parked in Mickey's personal parking space. He hadn't, as per his usual custom, switched his ride from Mercedes to Alfa Romeo during the lunch break.

"Greetings, master," Becca said, kidding. "You're looking very masterly this afternoon." Not kidding.

No hollows under his eyes, no stubble on his chin. He'd taken off his suit jacket and hung it on the coat rack as opposed to flinging it on the couch. Shirt sleeves rolled up, bare elbows on his desk. The very cliché of a sober, hardworking boss.

As long as the cliché was productive, she had no problem working with a cliché.

"Here's the Baker paperwork," she said. "Also the septic report on the Hutchinson place."

He looked at both sheets. Took a leisurely second look.

Mickey, laid back.

Would wonders never cease.

"So, the mall rally," she said, moving forward. "Should we hire a band? They could play for an hour or so beforehand, warm up the crowd."

"Which band did you have in mind?"

"Hadn't thought that far ahead."

"Make it the high school band," he said. "Donate to their uniform fund or whatnot."

Mickey not fighting her on campaign appearances? Making suggestions? *Helpful* suggestions? *Strategic* suggestions? She was ecstatic.

"Excellent," she said, marking the clipboard, already at the door.

"Before you go, just so you're aware, I'm hiring another receptionist."

Very short-lived, her ecstasy. She squelched a frown but didn't quite throttle the sigh. They didn't need another receptionist. They had Candy, covering the phones and the reception desk.

"You don't think Candy's doing a good job?"

"This isn't about Candy's job performance, good or bad."

"O…kay," she said, beginning to feel sharply otherwise.

Mickey hired no one. He left that "crap," as he called it, to her. So why this exception? And why hadn't she been consulted?

"I'm sending in the ad for our new properties tomorrow. I can write up something for the employment section and send that along at the same time."

"No need to advertise. She's been hired. Starts next week."

"And our new employee's name is…?"

"Leeta Porter."

"Leeta Scaff? The hospital receptionist? The wife you forbade me to lean on?"

"One and the same."

"Is she a crack typist?"

Because, although Candy was an excellent typist, two excellent typists would make shorter work of the paperwork pile. Much shorter work.

"I doubt Leeta Porter can print her name, much less type," Mickey said.

"So you've hired a receptionist who doesn't type."

"Don't blow a gasket. It's temporary."

"How temporary?"

"Temporary is all you need to know."

"I disagree."

"Let it go, Becca."

"I have to supervise this woman."

He put his hands behind his head, tilted in the chair.

"And you imagine being in on my little get-even scheme will make that job easier?"

He was smiling; she wasn't. She felt her neck go hot. Soon her face would follow suit and she didn't want Mickey to see such blatant proof that she cared about the shutout, about Mickey paying back a woman— and not a wealthy one—without her direct involvement.

"Couldn't hurt," she said.

"Oh, I think I'll spare you another Mickey-gets-pissed-on saga."

"Don't. Spare me," she said in a tone she wasn't proud of.

"Minor payback, Becca. Nothing for you to fret about."

But she was fretting—a fretting that increased as the afternoon progressed. Mickey's recent behavior now appeared less wondrous than ominous. No nighttime racing, no midday drinking, engagement versus indifference: symptoms she'd failed to identify correctly. He hadn't gone mellow. He'd just been biding his time, laying the groundwork, relaxing a bit before indulging—overindulging—in the pleasures of his newest revenge.

As soon as Mickey refused to let her hard sell the Bevin General receptionist, she should have realized he had other score-settling plans for Leeta Scaff. Her error, her failure of detection. And now a leftover grudge in the shape of a hospital receptionist had surfaced in the final months of the campaign. Last-minute scandals cost candidates votes, lost elections. No payback scheme involving George Scaff's wife was going to ruin Mickey's chances in November. That simply wasn't going to happen.

Before it did, she'd pay off Leeta Scaff herself.

TEN

Most of the people who knew George Scaff—relatives, friends, bare acquaintances—wondered why he'd married Leeta. Why join fates with a known rambler? A girl famous for fooling around before anyone in Mawatuck ever heard the term "free love." A woman, rumor squawked, who'd celebrated her curtain call to the singles' life, the night before her wedding day, in the arms of another man. Pregnant, had to be. Maybe by the groom, maybe not. And poor, decent George Scaff had assumed responsibility regardless, taking on Leeta Porter as his lawfully wedded wife.

Yeah, the busybodies of Mawatuck had a field day over his nuptials, and he let them. Didn't try to defend Leeta's "honor" or explain what no one wanted to hear anyway. He'd married and stayed married for love. Just that. After six months anyone with eyes saw that a baby—his and Leeta's or Leeta's with another guy—hadn't set off Porter/Scaff wedding bells. But that reality hadn't worked in Leeta's favor either. Those who'd called her a slut before just added "brazen" to the slur, the brazen slut who'd trapped poor, decent George Scaff.

Far from feeling trapped, he'd felt astonished and unaccountably lucky. Even now, he could hardly believe that Leeta had agreed to go out with him, much less marry him.

On their first date, a dance held in the gym, Leeta's formfitting skirt rode high on her thigh. On the way to the bathroom, she dropped—on purpose, he was fairly sure—her pocketbook and bending over to retrieve it stayed bent, fiddling with her ankle bracelet. His hovering buddies yowled, envying his good fortune: to be dating crackerjack Leeta Porter.

"The Scaff Man must be running himself ragged, just to keep pace. Just to keep it up."

During that smirk fest, he'd grinned—a grin that passed for confidence, he hoped.

"Knockers ain't bad either, bud. Just look at those mamas swing."

Nothing about Leeta approached bad, but the conclusion seemed too obvious to declare so he kept smiling.

"Guy's so sure of gettin' laid, he ain't even slightly worried."

"Had her so many times, already tired of that hole."

"Is that a fact, Georgie? Do you stand before us one exhausted bastard?"

Smiling confidently or otherwise only got him so far, so he cocked his eyebrows—both because he'd never learned to cock just one. Another feint that earned him credit for nothing he deserved. Cocking anything passed as proof that George Scaff was in *firm* control.

A crock, of course. If anyone was in control, it was Leeta. Before the band packed up, she suggested they "scram to beat the crowds."

"Sure," he said without knowing where they were scramming to or caring. Wherever, he was amenable.

"Know the way to Harry's Hump?"

"Sure," he said again and drove eighty miles an hour to get to that asphalted sand dune that doubled as lovers' lane.

It was at Harry's Hump, at Leeta's urging, that he first touched her breasts. During their warm-up kiss she opened her mouth and shot her tongue between his lips. Second kiss, she unzipped his fly.

Bet she's too fast for ole George, he thought he heard, although no guys at Harry's Hump would have been paying more attention to "the Scaff Man's" progress than to their own.

Mortifyingly, he turned out to be the speedy one. Jammed against the door handle, he should have concentrated on circumstances less electrifying to slow the rush, tamp the flow.

"What say we try that again," she said and proceeded to chew on his ear, casual about the blunder.

Lord knows he was willing. And the wonderful, startling part was: they did improve as a twosome. Their compatibility seemed to take her by surprise too. After a second go-around, with something like affection, she slammed a fist into his shoulder.

"And they told me you were a cool cucumber."

"The coolest," he said, at a loss as to what to say.

She reared back then, studying his face as if they weren't still bodily attached.

"You're not going to pretend anyone said the same about me, are you?"

A test, surely. He would have lied to please her, but he didn't know which lie would.

"Good," she said at his muteness, then giggled, vibrating them both.

Amazingly, he hadn't had to pretend anything with Leeta: not that he considered her the most incredible female around (she came close), not that he was instantly and hopelessly love struck (he wasn't). He was

146

interested—definitely interested—but far from presuming, on the basis of a dance date and Harry's Hump rendezvous, that they counted as anything close to a couple.

Leeta dated lots of guys, sometimes two a night.

He hadn't asked her out the weekend following the gym dance and she hadn't stayed home. Throughout the following week, communications were minimal: hi there's in the hallway, hi there's in the lunch line. Once she appeared at his locker and offered him a stick of bubblegum he had to refuse. The scent of bubblegum, even in the wrapper, made him queasy. Always had.

Once again she didn't seem particularly offended.

"See you at the pep rally," she said and off she went.

By then he'd more or less accepted that their night together was a once-in-a-lifetime hookup. With his buddy pack, he sat on the top row of the bleachers, happily razzing cheerleaders until she wedged in beside him, neatly dividing that all-boy block.

"You're all right, George Scaff," she declared.

"Yeah?"

"Yeah. Really all right."

When, how or why she'd reached that conclusion he had no idea, but to keep from jinxing what seemed like a compliment, he played along. In turn, she pressed her thigh against his thigh, grabbed his hand, and in the middle of a crowd of cheerleaders, basketball heroes and his dumbstruck sidekicks, put his thumb in her mouth and sucked hard. He turned to jelly, but he wasn't yet in love.

Even after he fell certifiably in love with Leeta Porter, they didn't date exclusively. She still rode off to the beach with athletes; he still escorted Beta Club blondes to the movies in Jackson City. Months passed before he and his date crossed paths with Leeta and hers. He'd been standing in line to buy two tickets to the nine o'clock showing of *True Grit* when Leeta and her date exited with the early show crowd. Done with movies and off to sandier destinations, he assumed. The guy he didn't recognize.

"This is Zeke," Leeta introduced.

Since Zeke wore a letter sweater decorated with three bars and two stars, only two of Zeke's teams had elected Zeke captain.

"You'll love this movie!" Leeta predicted.

His date pulled on his sleeve.

"Anyway," he said for at least the third time, "we were just going in."

"Bye," Leeta said, then dropped her pocketbook.

"Like everyone doesn't know she wears purple drawers!" his date complained to someone—maybe to him.

He'd already turned around, hand stuck in the slot to retrieve his change when Leeta came at him from his blind side. With remarkable force her mouth collided with his own, driving them both into the glass.

The ticket taker rapped sharply in warning.

"You hear me?" Leeta demanded, eye to eye. "Really all right. I'm not kidding."

He hadn't thought she was kidding; he also hadn't quite taken her meaning. Two-time Captain Zeke also seemed confused. Although the athlete missed the kiss, he had circled back in time to hear the commentary.

"What's this 'all right' business?"

"None of yours," Leeta said.

"I don't get it," said Captain Zeke.

"We're shocked," Leeta said.

"Hey, bitch! You making fun?"

Grabbing her arm, Captain Zeke spun her sideways.

"Hands off, jock!" Leeta squealed, yanked free, and took off. Within seconds she'd outdistanced the scope of theatre lights. Eventually Captain Zeke followed.

"Can we go in now? Please?" whined his date, the blonde standing beside him, a girl he'd completely forgotten.

Before declaring his love for Leeta to Leeta, George had auditioned in front of Beth—his good friend, Leeta's best. Drove to the trailer. Made his confession. Got as drunk at Beth's trailer as he'd needed to get to knock on Leeta's door.

Asked, Leeta said: "Why not?"

"Yes?" he persisted, head spinning. "You want to? Truly?"

"What is this? Some kind of trick?"

Not a trick, but he did long for a co-declaration of faith: in the future; in them—as a couple.

"You want me to say I hold marriage sacred, that kind of junk?"

"I just want to make sure you want to get married. Specifically to me."

"Jesus Christ! Most guys are happy with yes."

"Leeta," he said miserably. "Please. This is important."

They were then standing—she was standing, slouched; he was listing —in the driveway of her parents' yard. The moon wasn't full. Leeta didn't look her loveliest. He didn't, he felt sure, even in moon shadow, look like a fellow of substance or consequence, like anyone another anyone would be willing, much less eager, to tie her fate to.

She kept grinding her toe in driveway dirt, hands stuck in the back pockets of her jeans, face twisted toward the ground, not him.

"Can't we leave it: 'Will you marry me?' 'Sure, I'll marry you.' When I agree, I'm agreeing right now, this minute. Just like you're asking this minute. Besides which, I'm pissed. How come you told Beth first?"

Of course Beth had called Leeta—to help his cause, to make sure Leeta, caught off guard, wouldn't blurt an answer Beth didn't want spoken and he didn't want to hear.

"I thought you'd turn me down," he admitted.

"Liar."

"It's true. I figured my chances were less than fifty-fifty."

"Fucking liar," she said, suddenly more amused than peeved. Then she made a grab for his crotch and found his dick, happy to be found.

"So yes?" he said in the strained voice of the pleasurably gripped.

"I believe so, George Scaff," she said. "I believe so."

149

They married after the corn had been picked, with Beth the single attendant in a small church too large for their few guests. For her bride's day, Leeta wore the highest heels she could walk in. Coming down the aisle, she swung side to side as much as she swung forward, toward him. Her dress was bright blue. No one had been allowed to wear white.

"Because I fucking hate white," Leeta said.

It didn't matter to George. He bought what Leeta told him to buy, wore what Leeta told him to wear: blue shirt, blue suit, blue socks.

Beth's dress was bright green. When the preacher's wife mistook Beth for the bride, Leeta kept the misunderstanding going, hugging and congratulating her bridesmaid, repeating the preacher's wife's blessing: "May you live and love in the bosom of the Lord."

Beth wasn't amused.

"Come now, Lizzie Beth," he'd said. "The Lord and bosom in one sentence? Bears repeating, don't you think?"

"No," Beth said and shoved him toward the sanctuary. "Until you're standing at the altar, I can't go in and Leeta can't either."

So he took up his assigned groom's position and Leeta, following Beth, commenced her swaying.

No relatives from either side were invited to the after-wedding party held in and around Beth's trailer. After the first keg ran dry, a few of the fearless decided to swan dive from pine branches to the strains of "Sittin' on the Dock of the Bay." The evening's theme song, "Louie, Louie," didn't quite survive the night. Beth's record stack looked a little too much like a stool.

During the drinking and dancing, he and Leeta had gotten separated. He didn't remember falling asleep on Beth's too short couch, but there, with a crick in his neck, was where he woke, needing to piss. He looked around for Leeta, expecting to find her snoozing nearby, not too concerned when he didn't. First he'd piss, then he'd search. He high-stepped his way across the bodies that were clumped on Beth's floor, heading toward the pine break behind the trailer, a relatively private pissing spot.

And then whatever piss was in him must have dried up.

He saw the blue dress. He saw Larry Markham beside the blue. Sun coming up at his back, standing in dewy grass, smelling pine, he looked down and kept looking at what he didn't want to see. With her face gone slack in sleep, Leeta didn't entirely look like Leeta, allowing him to pretend for the briefest moment that the woman in the straw wasn't his bride. Then she shifted, arched her back, opened her eyes—no one but Leeta.

So the gossips got it wrong: Leeta spent their wedding night, not the night before, wrapped around another man. And he, groom of one night and half a day, found out because he'd needed to piss. Leeta wouldn't have "confessed," wouldn't have thought it necessary. As a boyfriend, as a fiancé, he'd never acted possessive or jealous. Why would she assume he'd change spots as a husband?

"Hey," Leeta greeted him her first morning as Mrs. George Scaff, pine straw dropping from her hair, her sleeves, some of it falling onto Larry Markham who also opened his eyes.

"George—shit!" Larry said, trying simultaneously to rise and run.

Sitting up, stretching, Leeta wobbled a hand in his direction.

"Lift, please."

He lifted.

"What time is it? Late?"

As Larry Markham scrambled across pine needles, Leeta curled her arms around his ribs, leaned into his chest, yawned.

"Think there's any cake left?"

"I think we can scare up a slice," he said, all he said.

"Great," said his bride. "Because I'm fucking starving."

"Hey," Leeta said, suddenly beside him in the shed.

"Hey back at ya," George said, setting aside the soldering iron. "When did you get home?" He glanced at his watch, speckled with metal shavings. Half past three. "Receptionist holiday?"

Rather than answer, she chewed her fingernails.

"What? What is it?"

He tried to make that query sound lighthearted, as if he asked only to prove he was paying attention. But his chest had gone tight. Leeta didn't go in for conversational drama. Not for its own sake.

To escape his reaching hand, she stepped sideways.

"You're not going to like what I'm about to tell you."

"All right. But while I'm hearing it, I'd rather you look me in the face."

Instead, she picked up and fussed with a pair of pliers.

"Okay. Here goes. I'm just going to say it. I've been offered a better paying job."

"A better paying job?" He whistled—to tease but also in relief. "Well, darlin', that is awful news."

"Stop," she said, shimmying farther away because he'd reached for her again. "You haven't heard who I'll be working for."

"Then spit it out. Who?"

"Mickey Waterman."

"Good one," he said.

"You think I'm joking?"

"Hard to judge since I've yet to see your face."

She gave in then, looked at him. A look of stubborn defiance. Anything he'd say or try to say would be a waste of words, an exercise in gum flapping. Leeta hadn't really come to the shed to talk; she'd come to declare. And now his role was to accept without protest. Protest was futile —that much he grasped. Maybe, maybe, he could have persuaded her not to work for Mickey Waterman, but to get his wife to turn down more money, from anyone?

He didn't wield that kind of influence. His husbandly authority didn't stretch that far.

Never had, never would.

They sat on the same lumpy couch, ate fried chicken from the same dented cardboard bucket, watched the same television program, but they might as well have been sitting and eating and watching in separate counties.

"You plan on keeping up this silent treatment forever or just till the end of the year?" Leeta asked, throwing a half-eaten drumstick back into the container. "You're not being fair. You know that, don't you?"

He didn't reply to that question either.

"George!"

"What?"

"Stop it! You're acting like a jerk! This whole cold-shoulder routine because—what? I'm taking a job that pays lots, let me emphasize that, *lots* more."

"Have I asked you not to take it?"

"You haven't asked anything! I could have pretended I still worked at the hospital, you know. You should be glad I told you."

"Those are my choices? Be glad you're working for Mickey Waterman or be lied to?"

"What does it matter if I'm bringing home a bigger check?"

"It matters to me."

She dropped to the floor, wedged herself between his legs, held onto his knees.

"George. Let's not fight. I really, really, really don't want to fight about this."

He reached out, rubbed her neck. She leaned into his touch. If he concentrated on that connection, their connection, just that and only that, could he shut out what he didn't want to think or talk about ever again?

"Don't you see? This is our chance," she said.

"Our chance for what?"

"For…more."

"But you're all the more I want," he said.

She smiled, brought her arms up to his neck, licked his nose.

But he hadn't finished.

154

"You and the farm."

"Oh, right," she said, leaping up. "Let's not forget the goddamn farm."

ELEVEN

Forty-six minutes past nine a.m., employment day one, Mickey's new hire strolled in—or so Becca gathered from Candy, who came tattling.

Candy Fenshaw took enormous pride in her job and performed that job admirably. But on occasion her insecurities gummed up the works.

"Thanks for alerting me, Candy," Becca said—a dismissal, and yet Candy continued to hover, anxious eyes desperate for an explanation as to why a second desk had joined hers in the reception area.

Even inclined to share, Becca had no explanation to offer. Mickey had hired Leeta Scaff on his own, for reasons of his own. She'd asked for elaboration; he'd declined to give it. As a result of that withholding, both she and Candy were going to have to play it by ear.

"Mr. Waterman was concerned about your increased workload because of the campaign," she improvised. "Neither of us wants you taking on more than your fair share."

"But I'm not, Ms. Denby. And I can do a lot more, if you and Mr. Waterman want me to," Candy pleaded.

Undoubtedly. But Candy already did plenty. The woman typed eighty-five words a minute error free on an IBM Selectric, answered a constantly ringing telephone and treated insufferable homebuyers with unfailing graciousness. Whatever Mickey's agenda, Candy Fenshaw would not be forced to take on more work to accommodate it.

That Becca guaranteed.

"Please ask Mrs. Scaff to take a seat in the reception area. I'll be out shortly."

Mrs. Scaff had been tardy; now Mrs. Scaff would wait in turn.

She checked with her sales associates; she made a bathroom detour. She adjusted her gold wristwatch; she smoothed her linen suit. She returned to her desk and the campaign map. She made a call, another. She massaged her right ankle. Only then did she pick up pad and pen and enter the reception area.

Mrs. Scaff seemed to have dressed as if competing on a game show—very, very, very brightly.

"Nice to see you again," Becca greeted. "Although we'd expected to see you earlier."

A rebuke, which Mrs. Scaff didn't hear, didn't process, or flagrantly ignored.

No matter.

Everything Becca needed to know about the new employee that non-response conveyed.

"You'll be working here." She pointed to the empty desk. "You and Candy have already introduced yourselves, correct?"

"More or less," replied Mrs. Scaff.

Sullenness didn't throw Becca off her stride. Not in the slightest.

"Rely on Candy. If you have a question, she'll be able to answer it. She knows where we keep every paper clip around this place."

Absolutely true, but also a bone toss to the insecure, who beamed.

"On the employment application, just fill in your social security number, address and contact in case of emergency. Skip the salary history. I understand compensation has already been decided."

"And don't think I'll work for a penny less."

"Of course," she said, all too certain they'd get no actual, productive, conscientious work out of Mrs. Scaff at any price. Abundantly apparent: the woman was a slack-off, born and bred.

"And where is dear ole Mick this morning? Why isn't he out here, welcoming me to the fold?"

Candy's cheeks flamed; hers did not.

"Mr. Waterman isn't in the office this morning," she said.

"Is that so? Off getting his face buffed?"

"Candy, would you excuse us for a moment?"

To continue their sparring in a less public place, Becca led the new hire through a back door and onto the posterior flagstone path. Squabbling on the front walkway of Waterman Enterprises would never do.

"Escorting me to my car so soon? Not that I'm against the idea of knocking off early…"

The only new car in the employee parking lot was an old one: a once-red Mustang repainted in patches, which reminded her of her first ride, the beloved Volkswagen Beetle. She held old cars against no one. Mrs. Scaff's mode of transportation wasn't, and wouldn't be, a source of contention between them. The single exception, most likely.

"Let me be explain a few things. First day. Upfront."

"Looks more like out back to me."

"You'd rather not talk in private?"

"Why are we talking, period? You're not my boss."

"But I am your keeper," she said. "Your arrangement with Mr. Waterman? Between you and Mr. Waterman. Your behavior as a Waterman Enterprises employee? My watch."

"What's that supposed to mean?"

"You displease me, you don't get paid."

"Fuck if that's so. "

"I'm a creative girl with numbers, Mrs. Scaff. Do you really want to take on the person who handles payroll? I can pay you, not pay you, pretend to pay you. There are so very many ways I can affect your income or lack thereof."

"And you think I won't run screaming to Mickey?"

"And you think Mickey will take your word over mine?" she retaliated.

Cutting short that to and fro: the appearance of Mickey's Mercedes.

Under the mistaken assumption that Mickey's arrival would count in her favor, Becca's companion swiveled a hip, triumphantly grinned.

"Becca," Mickey greeted on the walk by.

"And good morning to you too, asshole," shouted his choice of receptionists.

Mickey didn't slow, didn't turn, didn't in any fashion respond.

Once the boss's rebuff had time to sink deeper, sting harder, Becca wrapped up the chat. "Take the rest of the day to think over our discussion. Be at your desk by nine tomorrow. Not nine forty-five. Not five after nine. Nine. Do we understand each other, Mrs. Scaff?"

"As long as I arrive by nine, I can call the boss an asshole. Does that just about cover it?"

"Just about," she agreed. "Tomorrow. Nine sharp."

Then she went to find Mickey.

"You're giving me a raise," she said.

"I am? What for this time?"

"Keeping Leeta Scaff in line."

"Take the raise but don't bother keeping her in line," Mickey said.

"She's a disruption. A major one. For me and for the staff."

"She won't be here long."

"She's already been here too long."

"Time flies when you're plotting revenge."

"Mickey…"

"Leeta Porter stays until I say she leaves. That's how it is and how it's going to be. My fun, my timeline."

"Is this about sabotaging the campaign? Your way of throwing the election?"

"The campaign is your obsession, Becca. It doesn't rule my every thought."

"You'd rather an incompetent receptionist rule my every thought?"

"I'd rather you forget about Leeta Porter and go along your merry way."

"Then keep her away from the business and the campaign," she said.

"Relax, will you? Leeta Porter doesn't give a shit about real estate or politics."

"You don't know that."

"Oh, I'm pretty sure I do."

"Then, for the record: unless you're paying to have big tits on the premises, Leeta Scaff isn't a sound investment."

Mickey laughed. "You think it's about the big tits? Trust me, it's got nothing to do with tits."

Liar, she nearly accused.

"So enlighten me."

"We're done here, Becca."

"Having Leeta Scaff as an employee? Bad idea," she said.

"Last warning: I want your opinion, I'll ask for it. But notice: not fucking asking."

"Fine," she said and departed.

There were ways of neutralizing an incompetent employee—and the effects of that incompetence—without the boss's assistance or approval.

If Mickey could have his fun, why couldn't she?

Mrs. Scaff did indeed arrive on time, employment day two. To check on that promptness, "Ms. Denby" made a point of being in the reception area, 8:59 a.m.

"Hi ho, hi ho," Mrs. Scaff sang, skipping in, clutching a Mars bar.

"Friendly warning," Becca said. "From now on, finish your breakfast at home."

Mrs. Scaff shrugged.

"What's a working girl to do except eat on the run?"

Whatever Mickey said, whatever he intended, no Waterman Enterprises employee was going to draw a paycheck simply for showing up and snacking on the premises. Becca would burn money first.

She handed Mrs. Scaff a telephone book and a copy of their telephone questionnaire.

"This should take you through the morning."

"Good morning (afternoon)," Mrs. Scaff read in a Shirley Temple voice. "This is (name). I'm calling from the Waterman for Commissioner headquarters. May I have a moment of your time?"

"Any questions about the script?"

"Just one. How many hang-ups before I get to quit?"

"Any questions about the script?" Becca repeated more slowly, as if speaking to someone two leagues short of dim-witted.

Mickey opened his door, beckoned.

"Oh look, Candy!" Mrs. Scaff jeered. "The big boss. Is this where we fall to our knees and give thanks?"

Cheeks mottled, Candy continued to speed type.

"If you're more comfortable on your knees, Leeta, by all means assume the position," Mickey said. "Candy, hold my calls."

In passing, Becca picked up the telephone receiver and placed it against Mrs. Scaff's ear.

"Dial," she said.

"Got a call from New York about the Mangels property," Mickey announced before Becca had time to take a seat.

"Excellent."

They'd advertised the Mangels parcel as creekside—a stretch. But it *was* certifiably low-lying land and located close enough to the swamp to turn soppy after a hard rain.

"Which who from New York?" she asked.

"That stockbroker who flew in last month. Flying back for another look-see this weekend."

"Which means he's decided he *does* want to spend his retirement fishing out of a drainage ditch."

"A drainage ditch we'll sell him," Mickey said.

"With pleasure," she agreed. "When's he due?"

"Friday afternoon. So the usual. Wine, dine, close the deal."

"I can handle that," she said.

"I'm sure you could," he said.

A neutral statement.

Moderately neutral.

"Could, can and will," she said.

"Any particular reason you want to cover this yourself?"

She didn't lack for reasons. She just wasn't eager to remind him what they were.

"Am I supposed to guess?" Mickey inquired.

"No."

His chair creaked.

"Losing patience here," he said.

He was going to make her say it.

"Better not to be linked with New Yorkers right now."

He picked up a pen, rolled it back and forth between two fingers.

"You keep forgetting our deal, Becca. Business first. Campaign last."

Still nominally polite, still semi-restrained.

"Not true," she countered. "I haven't forgotten."

"So what's this bullshit about me not meeting with the stockbroker?"

"I didn't say cancel the meeting," she said.

"You just don't want me there."

A muscle in Mickey's cheek had begun to twitch, a giveaway twitch, his irritation fast compounding.

"Or: I could make dinner reservations for the two of you in Bevin County," she offered.

"Dinner reservations in Bevin to scout property in Mawatuck," he said.

"That way, a Yank comes and goes with no one in Mawatuck being the wiser, and we sidestep charges of screaming against outsiders while selling to them."

"And I'm supposed to care about such charges because…?"

Again he was going to make her state what she'd rather imply.

"It'll hurt the campaign."

He stood up. He circled the desk. He left less than an inch between her nose and his—the better to intimidate close range, she supposed. She was Buck Denby's daughter. Bullying didn't intimidate.

"This is your fucking spotlight, Becca. You installed it; you turned it on. Now turn it elsewhere for twenty-four hours."

"We're leading in the polls. By a significant margin," she said. "And I can easily take care of the stockbroker."

The sale wasn't that big a score. Watching this particular Yank sign on the dotted line wouldn't soak Mickey's shorts. If she realized that, eventually Mickey would arrive at the same conclusion.

"You and this fucking, fucking campaign."

"Over soon, boss."

"Careful, Becca. This Mangels sale falls through? It comes out of your year-end profits."

"That's not going to happen."

"Because you can pat your head and rub your stomach at the same time?"

"Pat my head, rub my stomach, count backwards, walk on water," she bragged, snatching open the door and very nearly colliding with an eavesdropping receptionist.

"Can I help you?" she inquired, all good humor vanished.

"Probably. I'll get back to you on that," Leeta Scaff sassed, flouncing back to her desk.

She glanced over her shoulder at Mickey, who showed no interest in what had just transpired. He'd returned to his desk and pen rolling.

Real or feigned, that indifference bugged her.

"Such a delight, our new receptionist," she goaded. "Every day in every way."

"Is she? Hadn't noticed," he said without looking up.

"Mickey," she tried again, but he quickly cut her off.

"Don't you have work to do, Becca?"

Always. And now that Mickey appeared to have granted full immunity to a certain eavesdropping receptionist, that workload had significantly increased.

For the August mall rally, as Mickey suggested, Becca locked in the high school band for a donation of new uniforms and reserved a bus and driver to transport thirty-five kids, trumpets, trombones, drums and the odd tambourine from Mawatuck to Jackson City, day of. She greased the palm of the S.O.B. mall manager, agreed that Waterman coffers would pay for mall cleanup before and after the event as well as cover the cost of additional security during. She personally made the rounds of the shops, ingratiating herself with store personnel by handing out complimentary spa and golf passes to offset any lost business qualms. She completed and filed the necessary "special fire permit" paperwork. She met with carpenters about the design and construction of the portable stage. And because the carpenter gang didn't jump at a woman's orders, she added a retired longshoreman to the payroll to make them jump and while jumping to carry out her construction specifications, nail by nail.

To make sure Mickey didn't sound like someone with a sinus infection, she spared no expense on the sound system. Without shouting Mickey had to be heard over shuffling seniors and rambunctious children, to come across warm and fuzzy in a venue sporting concrete underfoot and steel rafters overhead.

For his stage companions, she passed on anyone who'd held or currently held elected office, opting to surround the candidate with non-competitors: a mechanic, a nurse, a PTA president, a teenage Good Citizen. Behind that coalition: billboard-sized photos of Mawatuck geese in chevron flight and the candidate in a tilled field shaking the gnarled hand of a farmer wearing coveralls.

Difficult to obtain, that candidate/farmer photo. Very few farmers of a certain age wanted to shake a Waterman's hand and the candidate shared their lack of enthusiasm.

But she'd pulled it off.

Finally, she'd had to decide what and how much campaign propaganda to distribute before, during and after the rally. That calculation, and recalculation, cost her some sleep. Ultimately she settled on a four-pronged approach. A flyer on the windshield of every car in the mall parking lot. A small crew positioned to foist leaflets and campaign buttons on any shopper who kept shopping during the candidate's speech. Browser stacks of *Waterman, Commissioner* hats and flags on tables and benches throughout the mall and give-away hotdogs and ice cream cones wrapped in *Waterman, Commissioner* napkins.

Rally day, she planned to close the office at two; Mickey would take the stage at four. No later than 3:45, the Waterman sales team would swell the ranks. Since nine of ten polled respondents associated the word "water" with blue, Mickey would wear his navy suit and tie; she'd wear her navy suit and heels.

For Mickey's speech, she'd penned an aw shucks/hard "facts" combo —short, but not too short. Impressive, but not taxing.

As long as Mickey played his part, the mall rally would pull more of the fickle electorate over to their side of the ballot. And to encourage Mickey's full-fledged participation, she shared Leeta Scaff's rally assignment beforehand.

"Directly below you: Mrs. Scaff and a bag of confetti."

"Oh yeah?" Mickey said, amused.

She needn't have mentioned the confetti. As soon as she uttered the word "below," she had him.

"A fucking mall rally," Mickey said, once again amazed by the shit he let Becca talk him into.

"You'd rather give a cornfield speech?" Becca asked.

"How about no speech nowhere?"

"Oh come now."

"And by the way: you're having way too much fun with this mall thing," he said.

"Think so?"

"Know so."

She winked. "Then join in."

Far more juiced about this rally crap than anything he'd ever done to her in bed—or anything she'd ever suggested he do. But so what? There was getting off on sex and there was getting off on power. He and Becca knew the difference. It was one of the reasons they got along: they both preferred the prize behind door number two.

Leeta Porter annoyed the piss out of Becca—that was a given. Becca hated slackers the way he hated lily-livered punks trolling Ward Street. But the notion that Leeta Porter was causing Becca more trouble than she could handle? Laughable. Blind, lame and shipwrecked, Becca could put Leeta Porter in a chokehold twenty times a day. No question, no contest, no strain.

"So I'll signal the band for a drum roll, you'll hop on stage and take over the mike," Becca coached. "Remember, once you're up there, act as if you're chatting with the crowd, not giving a speech per se. Hit the points we talked about. Interact with the audience. If we're running long, I'll give you the high sign. Main takeaways: Mickey Waterman is accessible, concerned, willing to work on behalf of the voters."

Fucking eleventh-hour prep: that's where he and Becca always collided.

"Enough with the last minutes. You want me to show up, now till then I don't hear the word rally again. Got it?"

"Okay. But…"

Always a fucking but.

"…just so you know? In my world? No such thing as over-prepared."

"Becca's motto," he said.

"No," she corrected. "Lesson learned."

Becca's world, Mickey's world.

And the Jackson City mall? Who claimed that world as their own?

Worn-out farts using walkers, fat mothers dragging their mini-fats behind them. The place hadn't had an upgrade—structural or cosmetic—in ten years, if then. A dozen stores selling chewing gum, greeting cards, exercycles, cheap watches, cheaper shoes, crap, crap and more crap. Compared to this sticky, stinking, dilapidated hell, Ward Street looked like the Garden of Eden.

Mickey wished the fuck he was on Ward Street.

He wished the fuck he was.

"All set?" Becca asked at his side, clipboard in hand.

Drum roll, cymbal crash, and there he stood: looking down on a sea of sad-sack humanity.

"Isn't it true, Mr. Charley? After the fire in '42, your neighbors rebuilt your barn in a week's time?

"Five years in a row, wasn't it, Miz Dodd, you won blue ribbons at the county fair for your apple pie?

"And Mr. Sanders, am I remembering right? Didn't you once complain that tractor of yours was ornerier than any mule?"

Pretending to be "one of them," their neighbor, their fucking friend, exchanging "feel-good," "community-binding" memories with "supporters" Becca had bribed and strategically placed among the crowd. Acting like he gave a shit about "shared heritage." Pledging to serve as their obedient watchdog.

"I see you've avoided the words 'profit' and 'profiteer,'" he'd noted, scanning Becca's first draft.

"It's a campaign, Mickey. Truth's optional."

"So I won't be laughed off a fucking stage in a fucking mall."

"Not a chance."

"Since you can read the future."

"I can read this piece of the future because I wrote it."

Before they'd left the office, for the ten zillionth time, he'd said: "I keep putting up with this campaign shit, get elected and we don't see a substantial ROI, no duty to the electorate is going to keep me playing commissioner—you got that?"

"Got it, get it, agree. If it turns out county office isn't a money track, we won't waste time wringing our hands."

"You know what I think, Becca Denby? What I suspect?"

"All ears, boss."

"I think you cooked up this election to get me off Ward Street."

"Extra added benefit," she said.

Fucking Becca.

Never backed down, always got in her whacks.

While he stood onstage, lying his ass off, Leeta Porter, penned in by Waterman realtors, scowled below him, clutching a bag of shoved-in-her-hands confetti.

Should she neglect to toss those flakes when Becca ordered them tossed, woe to Leeta Porter.

Because Becca was also a pro at retaliation. And she wouldn't wait years to inflict it.

TWELVE

Their softball team came in third place for the season. They'd done worse, in past years, so Beth's sidelining helped the common cause, she figured.

Leeta insisted they celebrate.

"Celebrate third place?" Beth asked, bewildered.

"Why not? Third place is perfectly respectable. Besides, I want to party."

"Party with the people who played," Beth said.

"You played."

"Not the whole season," she quibbled, wondering why she made the effort. Leeta never gave up until she got her way.

"The injured get to party too," Leeta overruled. "Anyway, it's not a big party. Just the three of us. The old gang."

"Old gang" made them sound so...bygone.

"Now: if you had a choice between steak and lobster, which would it be?"

Beth had never been keen on food. Lately she'd begun to resent its necessity altogether.

"I don't know."

"Stop being such a downer!" Leeta ordered. "We're going to the beach and we're celebrating!"

Beth still had the telephone to her ear, looking out the window at the pathway partially blocked by corn. Stalks high, she had less warning of visitors approaching.

"And I think we should go to Blackbeard's," Leeta declared. "Expand our horizons. Whadda ya say? My treat."

Since taking the job at Waterman Enterprises, Leeta had been on a spending spree. Salon manicures and pedicures. "New duds" and "big jewels" for herself and "for any friend who'll *accept them*"—as Leeta endlessly proclaimed. Before Beth had refused Leeta's offers from lack of interest. Now she couldn't afford the distraction. Now she needed to focus exclusively on lying low, conserving her strength, stockpiling energy, in case from one second to the next she needed to escape the trailer, the beseeching Matt Spruill, run away from her home, run for her life, just run.

Outside the corn stalks shifted. She stepped back, away from the window.

"So we'll pick you up around five, okay?" Leeta pushed.

Monitoring the sway of corn stalks, she must have said "okay," must have agreed to Blackbeard's, to celebrating, to going to the beach.

"Well, geez. Don't burst a blood vessel acting so excited," Leeta complained.

"I've got to get off the phone now," she said, shaking.

"Elizabeth! Really!" the tuxedo rebuked, swishing His knees in mockery. "Look at yourself. At this hour of the morning. Quivering like a leaf."

If she could have, she would have traded places with a leaf.

Leaves blew away.

George drove; Leeta chattered. Beth sat by herself in the Mustang's backseat, wishing she'd brought along a beer for the road.

Inside and out, Blackbeard's was supposed to look like a ship. Mostly it looked like an amusement park ride with the odd addition of white tablecloths.

In the subdued lighting, Beth didn't notice the change in floor levels, missed a step in the step-down. George caught her as she fell.

Leeta twice demanded a different table, then corralled one of the waiters who'd been conspicuously ignoring their trio. Only Leeta had dressed in appropriate finery; she and George could have been dining on heat-and-serve fish and chips. They didn't look like a group who'd be ordering champagne from Blackbeard's cellars; they didn't, first glance, come across as the fast, bottomless drinkers they proved themselves to be.

When Leeta raised a glass, Beth raised hers. As long as they were drinking, she didn't care whether they drank to softball or athlete's foot. George kept up his consumption but offered no toasts. They weren't arguing, he and Leeta, but they weren't connecting.

"Next up, touch football!" Leeta declared.

"Not for me," she said.

"Come again?"

"Sitting this season out."

"You are not."

"Oh, but I am," she promised.

George said nothing. George drank.

"Beth! We need you."

"Because there can never be too many fumblers on a team."

"You don't *always* fumble the ball."

"Regardless," she said.

"Tell her, George!" Leeta demanded, irked. "Tell her she's being ridiculous."

"Touch football, Lizzie Beth," he said. "Chances are you'll survive touch football."

Which very nearly sounded like an old-style George tease. But not quite.

"George's right," Leeta said. "You won't have to worry about hurting yourself. No tackling involved."

"Do I seem like someone worried about hurting herself?" she asked.

And then they were back in the Mustang and she was pitching around in the backseat and then they were at the trailer and she was fumbling her way into night air.

"Thanks for the champagne," she remembered to say to Leeta who flipped her off.

George saw her to the door.

"Be safe," he said, which started her laughing. Door closed, lights off, Mustang gone, she continued to laugh and then she stopped.

She wasn't alone.

"I have to pee," she told the tuxedo.

"Don't tarry," He said. "I so enjoy pirate ship adventures."

Tonight, as she edged past His limelight, He looked less like a god, more like a…fox. A merging of prayer and paw. Because of the pointy nose?

On the toilet she had time to ponder, so she pondered foxes. She seemed to recall George encountering a red fox during his trapping days. In junior high and halfway through high school, he'd sold pelts. Then he'd quit. If she wasn't mistaken, a fox had made him give up the hunt and snare. If she closed her eyes, held onto the toilet lid, focused, maybe she'd be able to remember, beginning to end, the story of George and the red fox.

"You know which ditch I mean, Lizzie Beth? The one that runs the length of the back cut? That's where he and I came face to face."

On a cold morning. Ice in the ditches, frost on the field rows, a gray, low-hanging mist.

"Already had three muskrats in my bag," George said, "convinced it was my lucky day."

The fox caught in George's trap had been gnawing at its bloody paw, trying to gnaw free, but hearing an enemy approach went still.

The fog-laced ditch, the bloody fur, the creature's chest rising and falling, propelled by a panicked heart. From George's description, she'd been able to see and feel the animal's terror.

"I expected to be bit, reaching down to free it," George said. "But instead of attacking, he jumped clear of the ditch and ran down the field path. Only when he'd put a safe distance between us did he turn and give me a look. But that look, Lizzie Beth. I'll never forget it. Like that critter was trying to speak my language, explain in words I could understand why I shouldn't be trapping."

What should she have said in response?

"You didn't trap Leeta, George. You didn't. She married you because she wanted to."

But when she'd first heard the red fox story, she wasn't the authority on traps and trapping that she'd since become.

"Elizabeth, my pet. Sit," He instructed. "Tell me about your evening. Was there a band?"

As an all-seeing omnipotent, hadn't He supposedly been at Blackbeard's along with them? Hovering in the shadows or floating near the ceiling, monitoring the drinks and conversation?

Why bother to rehash?

A burst of wind rattled the trailer door.

She flinched, cowered.

"No, no, no, no, NO!" He objected. "Not that melodrama. Not that ridiculous tale."

As if she had control over which tales she did and didn't remember.

As if He hadn't prompted the recollection by turning into a beast.

As a third grader, Beth had been assigned "The Monkey's Paw."

Courtesy of speedier readers, she knew the plot in advance, knew that if she read the story herself she'd remember every detail—especially after dark.

To get out of the assignment, she'd timidly approached the teacher's desk. Asked, bangs hiding her eyes, for a special exemption.

"I dream too much," she'd confessed. "And my dreams seem real."

"It's just a story," the teacher dismissed, sending her back to her seat.

Nightmares were also stories, powerful stories. But as a third grader she had no leverage over teachers, possessed no refusal rights. Complete the assignment or fail.

To protect herself as best she could, she read the story early morning, before class. By distancing it from night, she hoped to distance the scratching at the door, the mangled return of the dead. Unsuccessful, those precautions. Her dreams expanded the methods and implements of danger, widened the territories of threat and harm. Accidents took place on logging trucks, boats, tractors, in the woods, at the beach, in the middle of fields. Returned from the dead: a drowned man, a burned woman, a young girl who'd fallen between tractor disks, her shredded skin flapping.

Beth's dreams were very inventive.

Every night a new victim, a different injury.

It had taken a long time to shake "The Monkey's Paw" from her dreams, to escape its hold and fright. But once that had happened, she assumed she was safe; that she could relax, let down her guard. She wasn't in the third grade anymore. She'd grown as old as the teacher who'd assigned the story. Adults weren't supposed to be terrorized by fiction, by TV.

The program's title made no reference to the monkey's paw. It seemed to be about a glamorous racecar driver and his elderly parents, beset by money woes. The TV mother found a keychain on the floor. Picking it up, she wished the dirty floor would clean itself. The next time she looked, the floor was sparkling, gritless.

Shuffling in with the evening paper, the woman's husband said: "You've been busy."

"No," said his wife. "It was a wish come true."

Then, right then, she should have made Leeta switch channels, left the room for popcorn or more beer.

But she hadn't.

She'd kept watching as the husband stroked the keychain, asking for cash. Kept watching as the insurance agent arrived with a death benefits check, courtesy of an accident on the track.

When the wife, stroking the keychain, wished her dead son alive, on the couch beside Leeta, she'd closed her eyes but couldn't close her ears. A car racing home. Rising wind. The hobbling gait of a resuscitated corpse.

"This is going to be *so* gross," Leeta squealed, delighted.

By stomping on the magic keychain, the TV father destroyed its potency just as the wife flung open the door. Left on the steps, fluttering: a red racing scarf.

Peeved, Leeta yelled at the TV.

To her, Leeta said: "You can open your eyes now. The stupid thing's over."

"Are you sure?" she'd asked, trembling.

"What a bunch of morons!" Leeta railed. "If you're given three wishes, what do you wish for right off the bat? Unlimited wishes!"

How many wishes would it take to make Matt Spruill forget who she was and how to find her? To keep him from showing up on her trailer steps?

She should have realized it would happen, that it was bound to happen. That one day, one evening, too tired or drunk or stupid or weak, she'd unlock the lock, open the door and see not only Matt Spruill on her steps but a fetus riding his shoulder.

And when it did happen, when that horror sent her crashing backward, Matt Spruill, Army man, emergency expert, rushed in, lifted her off the floor, bandaged her knee, and declared with the conviction of the righteous: "You shouldn't be living alone."

His contract with the Army was almost at an end, Matt Spruill announced. He could reenlist or return to civilian life. Work at his father's electronics shop. Marry. Set up house. Raise a family. He wasn't afraid of commitment. Was Beth?

It seemed an Army trick: shaming the weak into pretend bravery. Beth could imagine new recruits in Fayetteville attempting to rise to their superior officer's challenge. She could imagine their alarm.

In her state of alarm she went mute.

During his monologue, Matt Spruill referred to her as a "fine woman."

I'm almost twenty-seven and often coarse, she thought.

She hadn't intended to sleep with him again. It was just another example of giving up, giving in, giving way.

In her cramped bedroom, Matt Spruill loomed large. He took up all available space.

Because she had consented to another round of sex, he assumed she had also consented to marriage.

"We could have the wedding soon or wait until after my discharge," he said. "Anytime you want to, really. Just name a day."

Back in his boxer shorts, perched on the edge of the bed, he described the shingled house his father owned—theirs for the asking. It needed a little work, a "bit of TLC," but he wasn't afraid of work, he said. And as the unafraid talked, she pictured him armed with nails and putty. Repairing the broken, shoring up the collapsed.

Stepping back into his pants, he maneuvered carefully. Her bedroom, her trailer, didn't accommodate an Army man's bold and fearless moves.

She would/they would have plenty of room in the shingled house, he promised. Lots and lots of space—inside and out.

"There's a grapevine in the backyard. And a garage. And a huge garden. You probably know the house. The one across from Daddy's shop? I guess it's too early to discuss your job—if you want to keep working, that is. You don't have to, if you don't want to."

On sour sheets she pulled her knees to her chest, held them there, as across the ceiling flashed images of shingles, grapevines, garden paths.

The future, their future, as sermon.

For God so loved the world, Matt Spruill loved Beth Anderson.

"We'll have a wonderful life together. I know we will," he said before leaning to kiss the Band-Aid on her knee.

Elizabeth Jane Anderson: Matt Spruill's new mission—and cross.

"Don't say no. Say you'll think about it. While I'm in Fayetteville."

She didn't say no. She didn't speak. She could imagine never speaking again.

She got through the week, weeks. Cashing checks didn't require or depend on her feeling happy or rested. On minimal sleep, with a hangover and hands that shook, Beth could still perform her teller duties, avoid the wrath of the branch manager.

But teller duties used up only forty hours of a week.

She and George and Leeta no longer automatically spent Friday nights together. After their evening at Blackbeard's, she hadn't felt she could just drop by. She waited to be invited, and there'd been no invitations.

On Sunday afternoon, nothing else scheduled, she got into the Plymouth, drove to Dillon Sykes's barn. Unlike the softball league, there were no fixed football teams. Whoever showed up played.

A way to forget real life for an hour or two, touch football. Soon George would begin picking corn stunted by a dry spring and summer. By 5 a.m. tomorrow, Sandy Walker would be carpooling across the state line toward another ten-hour factory shift.

Another thousand lug nuts twisted, another two hundred mounted wheels.

Why did anyone keep going?

Why didn't everyone quit?

Leeta, who'd been so gung-ho about tossing around pigskin, was nowhere to be seen.

For George's sake, Beth hung around, watched what passed for fun, another Sunday on its way out of Mawatuck. George used to joke that being born a Cracker had one advantage: you looked like hell from the start. George didn't look like hell, but even playing touch football he looked like a worried man.

"Coming to Graff's?" he asked, game over.

"Rain check," she said.

Drinking in a crowd, with a crowd, felt like an ancient pastime.

"Then how about we head over to your house, just you and me?"

"Sure," she said.

Disinclined to welcome visitors, to group drink, she'd still welcome and drink with George. Always.

At the trailer they stayed outside, perched on the hood of the Jeep, staring toward brown corn.

"Almost combine time," she said.

"Yep. I was just sitting here thinking about the first time I talked up middle busters to Sandy Walker, Dillon—all those guys. I remember Sandy saying: 'Uh-huh, George, but how 'bout we talk pussy 'stead of farm equipment?'"

"That sounds like Sandy," she said.

"They thought I was a stupid redneck and I thought one tractor ride would convert the pack. 'No thanks, bud,' Sandy said. 'While you're sweating out hurricanes and drought, I'll be at the Ford plant with my guaranteed workers' comp.'"

"So Sandy Walker actually had a game plan. Who knew?" she joked.

Tried to joke.

Going through the motions.

Just going through the motions.

"Smarter than this one here," George said, tapping his chest. "Against change on principle, this boy. Hard-ass believer in everything and everybody staying the very same."

It wasn't as if she didn't share the preference. She'd just given up the fight.

He leaned back on the Jeep's hood, balanced beer on his belly, lowered the brim of his cap.

"Now that I've bent your ear, Lizzie Beth, return the favor. Tell ole George one of your tales."

"You've heard all my tales," she lied.

"A tale retold. Even better," he urged.

He wanted to hear a story about Leeta and that she could provide. She had no shortage of stories featuring Leeta.

"Remember the G.A.'s?" she asked him.

Pentecostals weren't supposed to be part of that Baptist clique, but Leeta had coerced the Girls' Auxiliary leaders into taking one in.

"Lots of memorizing and reciting, right?" George checked. "'Yea though I walk through the valley of the shadow of death'? 'Surely goodness and mercy'?"

"But to G.A.-recite, you had to be G.A.-initiated," she clarified.

Blindfolded, she'd been guided onto a slippery "plank" and taunted by a squad of G.A. veterans.

A pirate's ship, Beth!

Hungry sharks, circling!

One false step and you're done for!

"Now I know what Blackbeard's restaurant was missing," George said through his cap brim. "A plank."

"Be glad it didn't have a G.A. menu. Frog warts and mice intestines to start. Then I had to suck a lizard's thigh. The worm course came last."

Um, yum!

He'll slide down easy, if you open up wide!

Wider! Wider! Wider!

"My mistake," she told George, "was listening too well to the meal's prologue."

After sticking her hand down a "worm hole," she'd separated out one of the slimies, raised it to her mouth, parted her dry lips.

Quick! Bite him in two! Otherwise he'll climb back up from the inside.

When she started to gag, Leeta tried to help out, tried to save her.

It's only spaghetti. Chef Boyardee. You ate it for lunch.

"But it didn't matter what Leeta whispered," she told George. "I still couldn't swallow that worm."

"So what did Leeta resort to?" George asked.

"Shoving and punching. 'Quit crowding! Give the girl some room! Not everyone can eat with elbows poking her ribs!' And when that didn't work, Leeta knocked over the bowl. And when that didn't work, she threw a hissy fit. 'I said I saw it and I saw it! Beth ate the goddamn worm!'"

"Which brought the mama chaperones running," George surmised.

"Oh yeah. To prevent a second goddamn, they would have promised the little blasphemer anything."

George sat up, grinning.

"So Leeta twisted a few arms, and you went on to recite endless Bible verses."

"I did," she said, glad to see him grinning, unable to join in. "But I wished I'd never tried to be a G.A."

"How come?"

"When the blindfold came off, Leeta was furious with me. 'I told you it was only spaghetti! Why didn't you believe me?'"

"And what did you tell her?"

"Not the truth."

"Will you tell me? Now?" he asked, back to looking a worried man.

"Behind that blindfold somehow I'd lost faith."

George sighed, nodded. "It happens. Despite the best we can do."

Which meant George had lost faith too.

George, who never lost faith, whose unshakable faith she so depended on.

A surprise, hearing from Leeta—especially surprising for Beth to get a call from Leeta during banking hours.

Leeta was also at work.

"Down here at the hacienda," Leeta got out before a voice in the background reminded "Mrs. Scaff" to limit personal calls.

"It's an emergency!" Leeta protested.

A lie that apparently didn't fly.

"Come by the house later, okay? Say okay, Beth!" Leeta finished up.

"Okay," she said but dreaded the appointment, afraid of what she would or wouldn't find there, afraid of what and who might be missing.

When she entered the kitchen, the yellow wall seemed paler, bleached. But why wouldn't that be the case? Things aged; people aged; time moved on.

"There you are!" Leeta said, breezing in from the bedroom, bathroom, from somewhere, wearing a red kimono, her hair short, black and curly.

She probably looked startled because she was.

"I know! Quite the change, huh? But don't just stand there gawking! Take some weight off those bones! Have a beer!"

Against her own beer can, Leeta impatiently tapped.

"Sooooo? Ready to be impressed?"

Before she could answer, Leeta bounded off.

Leeta's scurrying made her want to keep very, very still.

Bounding back, Leeta carried boots.

"Aren't these nifty? I bought them for George, but do you think he's even bothered to try them on? Try to keep that man in style!"

Was this Leeta's idea of a Lush Life?

Was it?

"Now! Your turn!" Leeta announced and again disappeared.

On this return Leeta carried a music box inlaid with ivory.

"I searched and searched for one that played rock and roll. But this one reminded me of you too."

"You bought this for me?"

"Of course! Why not?"

She couldn't begin to explain.

Cranked up, the music box played a tinkly "When You Wish Upon a Star."

"What? You don't like it? It wasn't cheap, you know," Leeta bristled.

"No, I…I love it. But it's so…delicate. I'm afraid I might break it."

"You're not going to break it! And what if you do? I'll buy you another one."

She held it as close as she dared, seesawing between dumbstruck and waterworks.

"Are you crying? Cripes, don't cry about it! It's not even broken yet."

Flustered, annoyed with her, Leeta reared back.

"It's just a little something, no big deal. You're not required to be beholden for life."

But she did feel beholden: for the music box, for their once close friendship, because Leeta had stopped Jerry Banks from tormenting a Holy Roller, because for so many years Leeta had believed her, even when she lied.

"Besides which," Leeta continued, sweeping her arm across the boots and lovely, lovely music box, "this stuff? Low-end compared to what's coming."

"What's coming?" she asked, afraid again.

"Let's just say I'm pretty sure substantial money's going to start flowing my way real soon," Leeta predicted. "And when it does? Crappy kitchens, crappy houses, every kind of crap: gone and forgotten."

If Leeta wanted to forget, decided to forget, Leeta would forget. If Leeta left this house, when Leeta left it, she hoped Leeta would leave with George; that George wouldn't insist on staying behind. If she still prayed, she'd pray for those conditions and assurances, those blessings. People drifting apart continued drifting unless something extraordinary brought them back together. She had nothing extraordinary to offer Leeta. She had only the past.

"Thank you. For this," she said about the music box.

"Stop thanking me! It's nothing."

But it wasn't nothing.

It was a beautiful goodbye.

THIRTEEN

"Ms. Denby? May I speak with you a minute?"

It wasn't the minute Becca begrudged Candy, it was the timing of that Thursday morning interruption. She wanted to finish the draft of Mickey's newest speech. This one, if she had her way, would be delivered on Mawatuck County soil within eyeshot of the courthouse during the court's morning recess. Since she'd offered the owner of the adjacent lot triple his annual property taxes for an hour's rental, she fully expected to have her way.

"Of course, Candy. What is it?"

Candy hesitated.

Becca checked her watch.

Candy blushed.

"I'm sorry to bother you with this, Ms. Denby…"

But, she thought.

"But I thought you ought to know."

"Then tell me, Candy. Tell me what I ought to know."

"Yesterday, Mrs. Scaff…Mrs. Scaff was trying to get me out of the office at lunchtime," Candy at last disclosed.

Candy ate lunch at her desk. Image wise, it was a little too reminiscent of Mickey Senior giving transient workers ten minutes to wolf down cold collard greens in the field, and she'd tried to discourage the practice. But when asked to cease and desist, Candy had whined: "Please let me, Ms. Denby. I don't like to go out for lunch." Code for either: "I don't like eating alone in public" or "I don't like lunching in public—period."

Officially she couldn't condone Candy's preference, but if an employee was determined to donate an extra fifty-five minutes to Waterman Enterprises? Productivity was productivity—or had been until Mrs. Scaff interfered.

"As you know, Candy, we've always encouraged you to take the hour off," she said to cover Waterman Enterprises' collective ass.

"Oh yes ma'am. I know. I know," Candy agreed. "But I never should have!"

Vehemence. From Candy.

This was new.

"Suppose we start again. What happened yesterday between you and Mrs. Scaff?"

"It's so embarrassing."

She got up, closed her office door.

"It's just us, Candy."

"But I feel so foolish, Ms. Denby."

"I'm sure there's no need for that," she said, suspecting otherwise. "What happened?"

"Randy and I were supposed to go to lunch—at least I thought so."

"Our Randy? Randy Stevenson?"

As a broker, Randy Stevenson showed promise. As a romantic suitor, far less.

"Yes." Candy's blush deepened. "He left a box of chocolates on my desk with a note asking me to meet him at The Harborside. The note said he had an eleven o'clock showing nearby but that he'd be done with his clients by noon."

"Would you mind showing me the note?"

"I would if I could, Ms. Denby! I put it in my desk drawer but now it's *gone!*"

At least Candy got a box of chocolates. But what had Mrs. Scaff gotten for that outlay?

"And when I got to The Harborside, Randy wasn't even there! I don't think he ever meant to come! In fact, I don't think he knew anything about the lunch or the chocolates. I think Mrs. Scaff made the whole thing up."

"You've spoken with Randy?" she asked.

"Oh, Ms. Denby! I couldn't!"

"Did you take this up with Mrs. Scaff?"

"I did! But she just said: 'Men! Always changing their minds!'"

"Well, we can't argue with that, can we, Candy?"

She smiled: a reaction for Candy to emulate. Hysterics wouldn't help discover Mrs. Scaff's true motive.

"When you returned, was anything other than the note missing from your desk?"

"No ma'am."

"You're sure?"

"Yes ma'am."

"And when you returned, Mrs. Scaff was at *her* desk?"

"Yes ma'am."

"I'll look into it, Candy," she said. "Probably a misunderstanding all around."

Like hell, a misunderstanding.

Leeta Scaff was up to something.

What?

"Thanks for the update," Mickey said. "Now send in the conniver."

"Can I stay and watch?" Becca asked.

"Not today."

"Tease," she said.

"Try not to look like the cat that swallowed the canary, Becca."

"I told you she was trouble. Prediction confirmed," she said.

"Trouble or minor mischief? There's a difference."

"I don't like paying a salary to either."

"And I don't want your smugness giving my game away."

"Which is? I seem never to have been told."

"Send her in, Becca."

"One more question. Then I'm through."

"I doubt the fuck that."

"The game? Winding down? End in sight?"

"Soon. Now do your summoning thing."

She walked to the door, opened it.

"Mrs. Scaff? Mr. Waterman would like to see you."

"Guess I'm in and you're out," said Leeta Scaff, sauntering past.

Mickey signaled: no counterattack.

She obeyed. Somewhat.

Addressing Mickey, she said: "Before I go: quick reminder. That game we were discussing? Clock's ticking."

"Thanks, Becca," he said, the muscle in his left cheek twitching.

Her contribution to the fun and games?

Deliver Leeta Scaff to a pissed off boss.

"Wow. Inside the inner inner," Leeta Porter said. "Isn't this a treat."

Didn't have the fucking brains to be concerned despite Becca's obvious desire to slice up her guts and serve them with onions.

"Cigarette?" Mickey offered.

"Sure," she said, settling into the chair across from him. But she didn't inhale, just flicked ashes.

She probably assumed he cared that she deliberately dropped ashes on his carpet.

He didn't remotely care.

"So how's it going, Leeta? Enjoying your work here?"

"Enjoying the paycheck," she said.

"I don't think I've thanked you. For the confetti throw."

Didn't like that comment, not a bit, and the dislike showed.

"I aimed for your eye," she said.

"Then you missed," he said.

"Not for lack of trying."

"Initiative. Something we like to see in Waterman employees."

"Right," she sniffed.

"So what did you think of my speech?"

"Which speech was that?"

"A demanding sport, confetti throwing. Total concentration required."

"You mean the speech about Mawatuck's glorious past and even more glorious future?"

"That's the one."

"Heard it. Just didn't buy it."

"No? Why? Didn't I lay it on thick enough? Lie with sufficient gusto?"

So easy to dick with, Leeta Porter. So fucking easy.

She shrugged.

"Let's just say you were unconvincing."

"Really? Unconvincing? And how about your abilities in that regard? Consider yourself a first-class liar?"

That string of questions made her sit up straighter. Whatever Leeta Porter's deficiencies, there was nothing backward about her fighting instincts.

"Okay. Enough small talk. Why'd I really get called before the big boss? Took one too many breaks? Got reported by the candy cane?"

"Beats me," he said.

Leeta Porter lived fine with stupidity; she coped less well with hanging mysteries.

"Since you're guessing: care to guess what popped in my head the other day?"

"Wouldn't know where to start."

"Here's a hint: high school."

"Yeah? What about high school?" she bluffed, defenses way, way up.

"That mural that appeared on the gym wall. Remember?"

She remembered. The eyes told him that. As well as the stiff jaw.

"Leeta Porter doing the dirty with farm animals, as I recall."

"Stella Wallace couldn't paint a clothesline."

"Which Stella must have realized since she painted in your name. To avoid confusion."

"Good memory," she snapped.

"The best," he said and left it at that.

For now.

When Leeta Porter exited, Becca entered.

"So? Why did she want Candy out of the office? Did you get to the bottom of it?"

"Didn't mention it," he said.

"And why's that?"

"Because Leeta Porter needs to assume I don't give a fuck."

"And why's that?"

"So she'll try something else."

"Mickey…"

"Remove Leeta Porter from your fret list. It's under control. And tell Stevenson to meet me in the parking lot. We'll be taking a long, early lunch."

"And from him you expect to find out…?"

"How much Leeta Porter leaves to chance. Because once I know the percentage, I can have fun with it. Satisfied?"

"Getting there," Becca said. "And you?"

"Also getting there. And to hurry things along, I won't be locking my office door."

"Bad idea," Becca said.

"Not bad, expedient. And just to be clear? You won't be locking my office door either."

He left his chair, walked over, clipped her playfully under the chin. "Why so glum? Think of it this way: if I screw up, you get to step in, finish the job. One way or another Leeta Porter gets hers. I call that a silver fucking lining, any which way you look at it. Don't you agree?"

When Becca was pissed, her ass twitched.

Tit for tat, man. Tit for tat.

FOURTEEN

On the ninth of September, a Saturday, she, Elizabeth Jane Anderson, would turn twenty-seven. On Thursday, the seventh of September, after work, Leeta insisted on rifling through the trailer's only closet, the bedroom closet.

Almost like old times.

"Seriously: don't you have anything in here less than ten years old? I'm searching but I'm not finding."

Then suddenly Leeta's detecting skills improved.

"Holy crap!"

Brought forward into the light: a suede, fringed vest.

"What on earth made you buy this thing?!?"

Not a what, a who: Leeta.

"Are you sure?" Leeta doubted. "A brocade vest, maybe, but suede? I've never gone in for suede."

"That makes two of us," she said.

The price tag was still attached.

"Anyway, this?" Leeta declared, waving fringe. "Proof positive. We need to go shopping."

"We've been shopping."

"And how long ago was that? Besides, birthday girls can't look shabby."

"So who's coming?"

"Coming where?"

"To the birthday party you and George are planning."

Leeta stomped.

Beth had missed Leeta's stomping.

Silly, but she had.

"You'd better act surprised around George. He's sacrificing half a day on his beloved combine in your honor."

"When, where and who's coming?"

"I'm not going to tell you all that! It's a surprise party."

"Not anymore."

Again Leeta stomped.

When Leeta stomped, she looked like a kid. But Leeta wasn't a kid and neither was she. After Saturday, she'd be older still.

"Oh all right," Leeta huffed. "Since you've already ruined the surprise, I guess there's no reason not to tell. This Saturday. Here."

"A surprise party where I live?"

"Because I didn't think I could get you to leave your precious trailer and go anywhere else," Leeta said. "Case in point: shopping."

"I'll go shopping for beer."

"And cake," Leeta said. "I think we'd better have a second cake. And don't go demanding yellow roses. Because the cakes have to match. And the one in my refrigerator has *blue* roses. Blue roses and blue candles."

"No candles," she said.

She'd never liked birthday candles.

Because in candlelight, as in church, Aunt Grace didn't look like Aunt Grace. And every year, when the stranger above Beth's birthday cake urged her to "blow *extra hard*" to blow out all the candles, she deliberately disobeyed.

Blowing out all the candles seemed so…ruthless.

Ruthless and sad.

"No candles," she said again to Leeta.

"Yes, candles! Two cakes, each with twenty-seven candles."

"Which would make me fifty-four."

"I don't care! Each cake is going to have twenty-seven candles! On the candle issue, I will not budge!"

And what if she did blow out fifty-four candles on her twenty-seventh birthday? What did it matter?

Who'd live to be fifty-four, anyway?

Who'd want to?

"And you've invited…?"

"People."

"And is one of those people Matt Spruill?" she asked.

"That's it. My lips are sealed. You've got what you're going to get out of me. For the rest you'll have to wait and be surprised."

She wouldn't wait in suspense. The Army man who considered himself her fiancé would come.

Of course he would.

A hurricane, a typhoon, nothing short of a declared war would keep Matt Spruill from her birthday party. He'd come and she'd have to stay.

George had showered and changed but there were still specks of corn dust rimming his eyelids; he could feel the irritation when he blinked, so he resolved to blink as seldom as possible for the rest of Lizzie Beth's birthday.

Leeta had gone over to the trailer earlier in the Mustang. He drove the Jeep, loaded with their grill, a cooler full of meat and two coolers of beer.

Walking up, he heard the tail end of Leeta's pep talk.

"Now act the fuck surprised, Beth!"

First he kissed the cheek of the birthday girl, resolutely underdressed in jeans and a shirt that resembled the one he wore. Then he kissed his wife wearing a shimmery blue dress with tiny straps. Then, as instructed, he stepped back outside.

"Surprise!" he said.

"Look at you," Beth replied. "All slicked and shined at quarter to three."

"Goddamn it, Beth! That wasn't at all convincing. George, leave and come back. Beth needs to practice."

"Being surprised, she means," Beth explained, adding whiskey to her beer.

"George, go! We're trying this again."

He went as far as the Jeep, turned around, retraced his steps and, for a second time, planted himself outside the trailer door.

"He's at the door! Open the door!" Leeta shouted.

Which Beth dutifully did.

"Surprise!" he said.

And Beth replied: "Look at you. All slicked and shined at quarter to three."

"You two deserve each other!" Leeta said in her beyond-beyond exasperated voice. "Did you bring the grill? Did you bring the hamburgers?"

"Yes ma'am," he swore.

"Saved by other aggravations," Beth said, wobbly already.

As his wife ran across the yard to check, her high heels kicked up a pine straw blizzard. To escape that vision, he joined Lizzie Beth, who'd plopped down on the couch.

"I see you've got your fortification in hand, but where's mine?"

"In the fridge. In the cooler. In the closet. In the tub. Take your pick," Beth said.

"You mean I have to leave the couch?"

"Nope," she said.

She leaned sideways, across the couch arm, reached down and brought up a cold one.

"George!" Leeta shrieked. "I can't find the potato chips! You were supposed to bring the potato chips!"

"Miss Leeta's mighty keyed up today," Beth observed.

The thick drawl was fake, but not the slurring.

"Yep," he said, wishing he felt as drunk.

Beth played with the cord on the window blinds.

"You'd think it was Miss Leeta's birthday."

"You'd think," he said.

Although for the next six hours, Beth's party as excuse, he aimed not to think at all.

"I'd give Leeta my birthday," Beth said in her normal drunk voice. "If she wanted it."

"Oh I'd keep it, if I were you," he said.

A nonsense conversation to go along with drinking—yet Beth looked suddenly stricken.

"I'm not good at keeping things. But you are, George. You are."

He was pretty sure she meant that as a compliment. But what if what he was trying to keep didn't want to be kept? What if forcing the keeping was wrong—and selfish?

"Happy birthday to me," Beth sang out, then stopped singing and started jabbing at air. "It's *my* birthday, so *I* get to sing."

"Who you talkin' to, birthday girl?" he asked.

"*You* know," she said.

But he didn't. And it didn't matter. Not a bit. Lizzie Beth could sing or not sing, talk or not talk to anyone visible or invisible. She could hiccup, play the banjo, beat the drums, twiddle her thumbs, walk on stilts —whatever she wanted to do. It was her birthday.

"Happy, happy," he said, saluting her with his beer can.

"No saluting," Beth nixed.

"I'll do my level best," he promised.

Couldn't manage much else, but a non-saluting beer can—yep.

Designated chef, George set up the two grills, doused the coals with kerosene and struck a match. But as soon as Leeta decided charcoal smoke was tainting the birthday cakes, he, grills and his folding chair had to pull up stakes and relocate to the outskirts of the yard, next to the woods.

Leeta was overseeing the picnic-table food spread; Beth was in charge of music.

"George Elias!" he heard and turned to see the tunes girl hanging out the trailer door. "The speakers are in the windows. Let me know how loud is loud enough."

He imagined every wild thing in Celus Snowden's cornfields madly scrambling for quieter acres. Blasted, "Wild World" made even his big ears throb. Nevertheless, he gave Beth a thumbs up, shook his head at Leeta. Whatever she was shouting, he couldn't hear. Guests were beginning to arrive. In addition to cooking the burgers, he'd been ordered to direct traffic.

Leeta and her high heels came running his way. "Make sure everybody parks as far from the trailer as possible. To leave room for dancing."

"Do my best, wife," he said before she ran off again.

Through a fog of charcoal smoke, he didn't immediately recognize Stella Wallace and apparently she didn't immediately recognize him.

"Well if it isn't George Scaff."

"One and the same," he confirmed.

Stella stationed herself a little close to the grill.

"I'd stand back a bit," he advised but if anything Stella shifted closer.

"Sorry to hear about your mom passing," he said, flipping burgers. "Leeta said she wasn't in the hospital long."

"Long enough," Stella said. "I hate doctors."

So he changed topics again. Or thought they'd changed.

"How do you like your burger? Crisp or crisper?"

"Leeta probably loves doctors."

"Never heard her say so."

"Probably because of their fat wallets. Leeta loves money, always has. Used to return Christmas presents that didn't cost enough to suit her."

"Must have been before my time," he said.

Stella honk-laughed.

"Oh sure. Before and during."

He shoved a half-done burger into a bun, the bun into her hand, went off to get a colder beer, came back.

"Yeah," Stella resumed as if he'd never left. "We all thought Leeta had set her sights on a doctor. But I guess she prefers politicians."

She's married to a farmer, he thought to say. But didn't.

"I remember Mickey Waterman from high school, even if Leeta doesn't."

"Leeta remembers," he said to interrupt Stella's yakking. Mostly to interrupt.

"Working for Mickey, having lunch with the creep."

He picked up the spatula, scraped at bits and pieces of charred meat.

"Whole hospital was talking about it. Leeta dressed to the nines, middle of the day, for her so-called interview."

So Leeta had accepted the job from Mickey at a lunch that hadn't been a secret—except from him.

"Gone way over an hour, my friend at the coffee shop said. Most people eat in forty-five minutes. Or less."

"That so?"

He'd heard enough of Stella Wallace's mouth, of Stella Wallace's gossip.

"What say we time you," he suggested, pointing the spatula toward her burger. "See how long it takes you to feed your face."

Again she honk-laughed.

Stella Wallace thought he was flirting with her.

"Who the hell invited *her?*" Leeta seethed.

"Which her?" Beth asked.

There were females in every direction.

"Horse-face Wallace!"

"Oh. Stella. That would be me," Beth admitted. "Probably me."

She remembered thinking, on Friday, that if she, quick, invited everyone she knew, there'd be more of a buffer between her and the Army man.

"Sorry," she apologized to Leeta, then retracted. "No, I'm not sorry. It's my party, supposed to be mine. So I get to dole out invitations too."

Leeta wasn't pleased but wasn't arguing.

Why wasn't Leeta arguing?

"Okay, so don't tell George, but I invited a few extras too. When they get here, act like you knew they were coming all along. Can you do that, Beth? Can you remember to do that for me? And just so you know, I *didn't* invite Rebecca Denby but she'll show up anyway since she's Mickey's ball and chain. And before you start asking why Mickey and Rebecca would show up at your party, I'll tell you: because there'll be fucking voters here. And before you ask why I want Mickey here…think a second. People blab at parties. People come to parties and drink let secrets slip. Office secrets. Trade secrets. And when that happens…"

Listening to Leeta's endless speech was making her dizzy.

She turned, wobbled elsewhere, without correcting Leeta's mistaken assumption.

Not every drinker spilled secrets.

Some drinkers never spilled any.

Because Beth saw him—shorts pressed, shirttail tucked, gift in hand —before Matt Spruill saw her, she was able to duck behind a hedge of arms and shoulders.

But the party had barely started.

She'd have to keep up the turning and twisting and bobbing and weaving for the rest of the afternoon and evening. To avoid coming face to face, body to body, with Matt Spruill, she'd have to become a contortionist, an acrobat.

As self-proclaimed dance coordinator, Leeta went about pairing bank tellers with bank tellers, the tall with the tall, the short with the short. Sandy Walker, Leeta paired with Stella Wallace—to get Stella's goat, no doubt. Getting Sandy's goat while also getting Stella's? Icing on the cake, Beth guessed. By the time Leeta's work was done, every her and him at the party had a designated dance partner with the exception of two: the birthday girl and the Army man.

She and Matt Spruill were supposed to do their own pairing off.

Automatically.

Instinctively.

An "obvious" perfect match.

"Husband," Leeta called toward the grill. "Forget those burgers! It's dancing time."

Through "Telstar" and "Tears on My Pillow," George's dancing tempo never varied.

"Speed it up, Scaff!" Beth heckled, not to embarrass George—to fend off Matt Spruill.

Meanness, drunkenness—maybe one of those would keep him at bay.

"Shut up, Beth!" Leeta shouted back. "At least he's dancing."

And then Beth remembered.

George never danced in high school. While Leeta danced, he sat off in the bleachers, pretending it was all good, all fine, Leeta dancing fast and close with other guys.

In the time it had taken that memory to swell and deflate, Matt Spruill closed the gap between them. Running, she sloshed beer, joined

George and Leeta, turned their twosome into a herky-jerky threesome that George tried to accommodate, Leeta too, before her antics caused all three of them to tumble.

"Christ, Beth, give a warning, will you?" Leeta said, knocking grass off her butt.

On the grass, she felt less dizzy, so she stayed on grass.

But that was a mistake.

Freckled knees. Un-smudged tennis shoes.

"Let me help you up," he said, extending a hand.

Let me, let me, let me.

Shunning assistance, she scrambled to her feet, dashed toward a clump of fellow drunks who were attempting to build a human pyramid and kept going, trying to get to her private reserves, trying to get to another drink.

But the cooler lid jammed between the wall and couch arm.

Because the trailer was small.

Because she was rushing.

She heard the latch turn, saw the door fill with a box tied with multiple bows and ribbons, saw the man who held it.

"Hi," he said.

If she'd been utterly sober, getting away, getting past him, would have been a feat, and she was nowhere near that.

"I've been wanting to give you this," he said.

"Oh," she said. A stringy orphaned *oh* she gave no mate.

"I bought this before we got…engaged," he stammered. "So it's not really as grand as…" He looked at his feet.

"No need to apologize," she said.

Because once apologies began, how and where would they ever end?

"I just didn't want you to open it, expecting something better," he said.

Expect? She had no expectations.

"I just didn't want you to be disappointed," he said.

She took the present with her free hand, placed it on the table with the others.

He retrieved it.

"Don't you want to open it now? I'll hold your beer."

They sat on the couch, his gift on her lap, her beer warming in his hand.

Unless she opened his gift, he might never leave the couch. He might grow into it, attach to its cushions, become the man who became her living room couch.

So she untied the ribbons, separated the top of the box from the bottom, pushed aside star-spangled tissue paper.

"Not quite sweater weather, I know," he said.

A cardigan with pearl buttons. Yellow.

Why?

Why had he bought this particular sweater in this particular shade of yellow? Why had he bought this particular sweater in this particular shade of yellow *for her*?

She searched his eager, eager face.

"If you don't like it, I can exchange it," he said tentatively. "I kept the receipt."

Her turn to speak.

And what was she to say, to do?

Congratulate him on his eerily accurate guesswork?

Acknowledge the perfect color match: baby sweater, mother sweater?

"You don't have to exchange it," she said—to fill the silence, to silence silence, nothing more.

But it gave false hope, that response.

"Then you like it?"

"Yes."

A dangerous word to say to Matt Spruill.

"So I was thinking, before I leave for Fayetteville tomorrow, you and I could…"

Plans.

In exchange for one *yes*, an onslaught of plans.

He wouldn't stop short of consent. He wouldn't stop. Already she'd been suckered into a yes. Already she was sitting next to him, holding his yellow sweater against her belly. Already Matt Spruill was making plans that involved her. Eventually Matt Spruill's plans would involve starting a family, having a baby. A baby who'd need a mother's protection. *Her* protection.

Another baby she'd fail.

"Oh please," Leeta begged. "Just me and you this time. No crazy-ass Beth."

"All danced out, darlin'," George said, but she wrapped her arms around his neck anyway, pulling him to and fro as gnats swarmed.

The coals in the grill glowed weakly. Burgers gone, beer almost gone, celebrations petering out in buggy twilight, he looked over Leeta's bare shoulder and saw the arriving Mercedes.

Rebecca Denby he hadn't seen since high school, but she'd stayed high school tiny. Only a woman that size could make Mickey Waterman look big in comparison. But at this darkening hour and stage of partying, Mickey looked plenty substantial.

When he stopped even pretending to dance, Leeta twisted on her high heels, saw what he saw.

And then his wife forgot him.

"Well look who fucking deigned to show. People invited to a party usually have the decency to arrive before it's over."

"George, good to see you," Mickey said and only then: "Apologies, Leeta. Becca and I had a business meeting. Couldn't get away sooner." And then again to him: "You remember Becca?"

Rebecca Denby put forth her hand, so he shook it.

"It's been awhile," she said.

"It has," he agreed.

Mickey held up a bottle of champagne. "For the woman of the hour," he said, "if you'll just point me in her direction."

"Why not drink it yourself?" Leeta egged. "Catch up with the rest of us."

"Beyond my reach, I'm afraid," Mickey said lightly.

Rebecca Denby said nothing.

"I believe there's some cake left. Would either of you care for a slice?" he offered.

"I'd love some cake," Rebecca said to him. To Leeta, she said: "Care to show me the way?"

"How hard can a picnic table be to find?" Leeta snapped.

"Can I bring you anything, Mickey?" Rebecca asked, taking the bottle of champagne with her.

"A beer would taste good, Bec. No cake. Thanks."

Very soon three of the four of them would choke on cordiality.

Leeta's hands were on her hips, legs squared as if bracing for an attack—or ambush.

He couldn't make sense of it: Leeta's surliness, Mickey's forbearance. Treating the man who signed her paycheck with the same contempt she'd shown the hood in high school—and getting away with the insolence.

Mickey glanced around. "Looks like Celus Snowden's got another few days of work in this field."

"Yep," he said.

"Tough year for corn," Mickey said.

Maybe because he couldn't see Mickey's expression clearly in twilight, that statement sounded sympathetic—almost as if Mickey Waterman counted as a struggling farmer himself.

"There've been better," he said.

"You can stop politicking," Leeta said. "You'll never get George's vote."

Mickey laughed. "Never expected to, Leeta. Which makes me appreciate all the more George letting you work in my office and on my campaign."

"What the fuck is that supposed to mean? George *lets* me."

"Leeta makes up her own mind about things," he said.

Not to applaud his wife's independence. Not to give credit where credit was due. He'd never been as noble or as honorable or as chivalrous as everyone seemed to think he was. He said what he said to clarify. He hadn't been consulted about Leeta's career move. He hadn't known a career move was in the works. Stella Wallace knew more about his wife's business than he did. So why not own up to the obvious to Leeta's new boss? He was just Leeta Porter's poor, poor, out of the loop, in the dark husband.

"Good to know," Mickey said.

And then Rebecca Denby returned with cake.

FIFTEEN

"Announce we're doing a dry run of the courthouse nonsense," Mickey decreed.

A dry run of a political rally? To throw off their timing, stall momentum, diffuse excitement, give critics a chance to critique twice?

"We don't need a dry run," Becca replied.

"But the candidate wants one. So arrange it."

"Not a smart move, Mickey."

"I ask for one thing in this fucking load of campaign shit and you make an argument out of it? Just do it."

She doodled on her clipboard.

"Did you hear me?"

"I heard you."

"So why aren't I hearing: 'Sure, Mickey. Yes sir, Mickey. On it.'"

Because she never called him *sir*, for starters.

"Because I'm waiting for an explanation that convinces me a dry run won't damage your, as you put it, fucking campaign."

"Do it, Becca. I want the office cleared out on Tuesday afternoon."

"You want the office closed? Fine. We'll close the office. We don't need a dry run."

He glared at her.

She was used to Mickey's glares.

"Then come up with another excuse," he said. "But get everyone out except Leeta Porter. Leeta Porter stays. Give her whatever the fuck job you usually give her and make sure she understands she'll be here alone."

Yet another bad idea.

She opened her mouth; he held up his hand.

"You want her out of your hair? After next Tuesday, Leeta Porter will be out of your hair."

The entire staff losing half a day's work to get rid of one slacker? Why not just fire her, effective immediately? But arguing Leeta Scaff with Mickey, as had been exhaustively and exhaustingly proved, was wasted effort. Time to cut her losses. If they'd truly be rid of Mrs. Scaff after Tuesday, then...hooray. She looked forward—immensely—to Wednesday.

"Just satisfy my curiosity about one little thing. Is this a George Scaff payback too? Because he refused to sell?"

During their birthday party drop-in, she hadn't expected to feel sorry for anyone there. And yet she had. For George Scaff.

"I've got nothing against George. His head's stuck in the sand, but he's a good guy."

High praise, coming from Mickey. High praise indeed.

But even without Mickey gunning for him, she couldn't foresee a happy ending for George Scaff, Mawatuck small farmer, 1978, economics and a wife named Leeta working hard against him. Mickey might keep his hands off George Scaff's farm. But farm and wife? That would require Mickey to curb not one desire but two.

Never had she known Mickey to exercise double restraint.

Never.

"So after Tuesday, no more Leeta Scaff?" she double-checked.

He nodded.

"And you realize, now that you've said it, I intend to hold you to it?"

"I realize," he said.

"Then rest assured: by 12:30, Tuesday, Leeta Scaff will be here by her lonesome."

"Not quite," he said.

She didn't act surprised because she wasn't.

"Leeta Scaff will think she's alone."

"Presuming Leeta Porter thinks," Mickey said with a notable lack of concern.

Which meant his retaliation plan didn't hinge on the receptionist's mental prowess.

Another non-surprise.

Ever true to her word, Becca cleared the office of all but one by 12:30.

Then Mickey made his noisy, conspicuous exit.

He didn't bother driving farther than the site of the old vegetable stand before driving back. As soon as the left-behind receptionist escaped Becca's guard, she'd leave the receptionist desk.

When he returned, he parked on the windowless side of the building, let himself in through the realtors' back entrance. He didn't stomp this time—but he didn't creep.

Leeta Porter had left the door to his office wide open, which left her wide ass in plain sight. While he stood on the threshold, five feet away, she continued to rummage through the papers on his desk for fake bills of sale, rigged maps, notarized confessions of robbery—something worth her blackmailing while.

Like he'd leave anything incriminating on his fucking desk. Anyone with a slice of brain would be trying to break into his personal file cabinet.

For a minute more he took in the broad view from behind. Then he got bored.

"Knock, knock," he said and she jumped, tipping over the desk lamp.

"Rebecca said I should look in here…"

"Did she?"

"Ask her, if you don't believe me," she stalled.

"Sure. Let's go ask Becca. Together."

Her hand went for her mouth.

"Now it dawns," he jeered.

Her teeth let go a fingernail.

"Fucker," she said.

"Mistake," he said.

"Asshole," she said.

"Mistake," he said.

"Stop saying mistake."

"Why? Because you want me to stop? Because it bugs you? Let me explain how this works. To the receptionist caught snooping in my office,

221

I get to say and do whatever I please." He paused. "Unless you'd rather I take you to court? Call George? Chat with him about the trouble his greedy wife got into today?"

"Keep George out of this."

"Oh, so now we're bargaining? Okay. I'm a businessman. What do I get for keeping George 'out of this'?" He waited for an answer, but not for long. "What's the matter, Leeta? Having trouble deciding which you want more, money or a husband?"

She stood there like the retard she was, saying nothing, confirming what he should have expected: she wasn't going to contribute her fucking share. All on him, making this interesting.

So he kicked it up a notch.

"Feeling nostalgic?" he asked once he got her into the Alfa Romeo.

Before she could say what, huh or duh, he spun them out of the parking lot onto 178. Once the speedometer's needle hit 95, he hit the brakes, pitched her toward the windshield, then played with the gas, teasing the pedal up and down, gear shift in neutral.

"Are you trying to kill me?" she squalled.

"From here to West End Road in under ten. Care to bet?"

"No."

"What happened to risk taker Leeta Porter? Guts crawled up her ass?"

"Leeta Porter *Scaff*. How hard is that to remember?"

"Call me sentimental. No matter how many Scaffs you marry, you'll always be Leeta Porter to me."

The Alfa shimmied in place.

"You don't scare me," she said.

"Those gnawed fingers say otherwise."

He took the last turnoff without braking. The road was dry. The Alfa kept traction. They skidded; they didn't flip. But he'd succeeded in making her smell the way he'd smelled, trapped in the Corvair, waiting to get punched and pounded.

On West End Road, mid-curve, across from the woods, he glided to a stop, easing off the gas—to fuck with her head. She'd braced for another brake slam.

"Get out," he said.

"Here?"

"Get out."

She was gripping the seat with both hands, counting on that hold to save her.

"Get out or get dragged out. I know how that's done. I've been shown. Remember?"

"No."

Lying bitch.

"This road. This spot. A Saturday night party. Main attraction: bait and beat a hood. Coming back to you now?"

"No."

"A roadblock? A Corvair? A gash in sandals kicking gravel?"

"That wasn't me," she sniveled.

"Your date kept calling your name, but you didn't want to leave the show. The hood hadn't bled enough to suit you. You wanted to see him bleed some more."

"I said that wasn't me."

"Want to know what gave you away? Even before your idiot date called your name?" He reached down, tapped her ankle bracelet. "The one you wore that night was cheaper, but even cheap-ass jewelry sparkles in headlights."

He waited for her to gather her wits, fight back.

Then he got tired of waiting.

"A little long in the tooth to still be wearing ankle bracelets, don't you think? But appropriate. Since a hood's now in charge of your fate."

She got the fuck out then, rushed toward the middle of the road, frantic to flag down another car, someone to rescue her from Mickey Waterman.

At his leisure, he also got out, leaned against the fender, extracted the first cigarette from a new pack.

"No use, Leeta. I can tell you from experience: not a lot of Good Samaritans cruise West End Road."

"People will be wondering where I am. George will be."

"Shall we swing by your house while we're out and about? Let the hubby know you'll be working late? I'm sure he'll understand. George Scaff has always been an understanding man as far as you're concerned. Very understanding."

"He won't understand kidnapped!"

"Kidnapped? This waltz down memory lane? You and me remembering old times?"

Now she ran.

He caught her easily enough, flung her back into the car.

"Did you think we were done? Because that would be another mistake: thinking we're done."

"You don't scare me," she tried again.

"Oh but I do," he said. "And for good reason. This party we're having? Right here, right now? Mickey Waterman's not the entertainment for this one. You are."

In her place, from the passenger seat, he'd have made a grab for the steering wheel, clawed at his eyeballs, sunk teeth into his thigh. Fought harder, dirtier.

He'd expected Leeta Porter to be tougher.

Stupid, but tough.

"Want to know where we're headed now—or would you rather be surprised?"

"Like you'd tell me where."

"Happy to. My house," he disclosed.

She'd assume he meant the white brick ranch with the bar and pool and water views.

As they passed his Oak Park driveway, she turned full around in her seat.

"I thought we were going to your house," she whined.

"My *old* house. Since we're reminiscing."

At Senior's caving in mansion, he didn't have to force her from the car.

"After you," he said, opening the front door.

"Nice pad." She smirked. "Did you pack us a picnic?"

Completely recovered from her West End Road panic. From being caught red-handed at his desk. From being shoved against her will into his car—twice. In the boyhood home of bowlegged, pockmarked Mickey Junior, school pariah, Leeta Porter felt surer of herself with every step.

"Thanks," he said. "I'm thinking of making it a shrine."

"To Brylcreem and zits?"

"Why not? Wanna be the tour guide?"

"When hell drips," she said.

"But think of all the fun you could have with the commentary. 'Welcome to the house where Mickey Waterman grew a pair.' Or: 'You all remember the runt who needed boots with heels to give himself another fucking inch.'"

Two line feeds, that's all it took to lure her in.

"A runt with tattoos. Don't forget the tattoos."

"Brylcreem, boots, tattoos, zits. Anything else?"

"What is this—a test?"

"Just making sure we're not leaving out any essential details."

"Because?"

"Because that's the guy I want in your head as you strip."

Confused, Leeta Porter looked stupider.

"Lose the clothes," he said, expecting a bit of a delay. Leeta Porter tussling with scruples, or pretending to. But that wasn't the holdup.

"How much?"

"How much of a strip?"

"How much will you pay me?"

He could feel his cheek start to twitch.

"Quick review: I caught you sneaking around my office."

"So? That's all you caught me at."

"Try to grasp the concept. You were in my private office, looking to find dirt on me. By catching you in the act, I now have dirt on you. Which means I set the terms of payment. My silence for your... compliance."

"You want to see me naked," she said.

"I want you naked," he clarified.

Leeta Porter assumed naked would play to her advantage. Assumed, in the buff, she'd have all the power, all the control. His dick at her mercy. His dick her toy. Horny bastard Mickey Waterman wouldn't stand a chance.

She jerked a hip in his direction, tickled a button.

Already he was losing interest.

"The standard bump and grind or shall I improvise?"

Leeta Porter peek-a-boo-ing her nips made him miss Ward Street. It made him miss the professionals.

"I should have figured this is what you were after all along," she said, squirming out of a hideous pair of purple drawers. "You never cared what I was doing in your office. It was just an excuse to get me to do... this."

"Oh I cared," he said. "But this is riveting too."

Just not in the way he'd expected to be riveted while inflicting payback. Leeta Porter was proving to have less of a conscience than he had. Revenge required a victim—not an accomplice.

"Now what?"

"Get on your hands and knees."

"Ah. So the man is particular."

Not that placement helped.

Besides too much ass, Leeta Porter had too much tit, too much belly, too much mouth. Her bush overgrew her twat, curled down her inner thighs.

"You wanted to fuck me in high school," she said.

"I did," he agreed. "In high school."

"You've always wanted to fuck me," she said. "You and every other guy."

Another pane had fallen out of the side window since his last visit, granting kudzu another entry. Another hunk of pig trough had rotted off. He heard the crow before he saw it, swooping past the porch railing, diving down to pick up something shiny. A bright, shiny mystery from the air turned bright, shiny disappointment up close. Nothing but wasted effort: the dive down, the ground search. Nothing new and tasty in its mouth, nothing to show for its trouble, the crow cut its losses, flew elsewhere.

When he turned again toward Leeta Porter he hoped he wouldn't feel as fucking bored as he'd felt before turning away.

But he did.

He fucking did.

He picked up her clothes, tossed them at her.

"Don't come back to the office. Becca will mail your final check."

"That's it? This is all you wanted? A strip show???"

She could walk home or crawl. Hitchhike, dressed or naked. She could spend the night in Senior's pig trough for all he cared.

A colossal waste of rage, getting even with Leeta Porter.

A fucking dead end.

If he got to Ward Street before he died of boredom, he'd buy a race. And if he couldn't get a fucking punk from Ward Street to follow him to Swampside, he'd fucking race himself.

SIXTEEN

Beth might have written a farewell note to Matt Spruill, left it pinned to his never-worn sweater gift. But to what purpose? To apologize for her departure? She wasn't sorry. To offer best wishes? Why bother? Quite apart from her wishes, Matt Spruill would thrive because success depended on effort and his effort was unflagging.

She sponged the utensil drawer and kitchen sink, cleaned out the refrigerator. Along with moldy cheese and sliced bread, she threw away mousetraps, rusty cans of bug spray, limp fly swatters. She owned no knickknacks, so she was spared sifting through porcelain shepherdesses and mementos from the Washington Zoo. She Windex-ed the television screen, two lamp bases, the trailer's windows on the inside. She trashed the mildewed shower curtain, two unopened boxes of Desert Flower talcum powder, the contents of her medicine cabinet. She bundled blouses, t-shirts, jeans, socks, sneakers and records into garbage bags. What wouldn't burn in the barrel behind the trailer, she left propped beside it. The rest of the beer, the rest of the liquor, the rest of everything.

Just after 9 p.m., she vacuumed. At 9:23 she finished mopping the eight squares of linoleum that fronted the kitchen sink. Her last pass through, she saw on every surface, in every cubby, emptiness where there had been clutter, tidiness where there had been mess.

She opened the windows, unplugged the phone, shut off the water and the electricity. In the dark, she picked up the four things she had set aside: car keys, Leeta's music box, the smaller yellow sweater and matching bonnet. Cash she carried in her pocket.

Leaving the trailer, without effect, she flipped the switch to the outdoor light.

Habits died harder than flesh.

At the 7-11, she filled the Plymouth's gas tank.

Tommy Constantine was working the night shift. He took her gas money, tried to sell her a case of beer as well.

"Good price," he coaxed. "Better reconsider."

"No thanks," she said. "Not tonight."

Would his be the last face she saw? Tommy Constantine the last person she spoke to, who spoke to her?

If so, that wouldn't be so awful. As part of Jerry Banks's gang, Tommy had watched her refuse to roll on schoolyard gravel, borne witness to her steady resistance. Which meant that Tommy would have a point of reference, a standard of comparison. He'd be able, from past experience, to confirm her last intentions. He'd be able to vouch that this night Elizabeth Jane Anderson had chosen to roll the Plymouth, had acted of her own accord.

"Not slowing down, I hope," he said.

Drinking, he meant. Buying beer *from* him to drink. Tommy Constantine was worried about losing his best customer.

"Not quite."

A plausible response to his remark.

"Okay then. See ya," he said.

She didn't say "yeah," drew the line at "yeah." Because yeah would have been a blatant lie and she didn't want the last word she ever uttered to be a lie.

A genuine last wish.

Genuine—and ridiculous.

SEVENTEEN

When George rose to answer the persistent knocking, Leeta, half-awake, objected.

"What time is it? Where are you going? Come back to bed."

He shifted the curtain, looked through the bedroom window. Moonlight alone wasn't bright enough, strong enough, to identify whoever stood on their shadowed porch knocking.

Leeta kicked off the sheet. "Who is it? Who's out there?"

Trouble, he thought to answer. What other kind of news would a post-midnight, pre-dawn visitor bring?

He pulled on his jeans, went to the door bare-chested, flipped the porch light switch.

Mickey Waterman stood on the other side of the threshold, blood on his hands, blood on the cuffs of his jacket, blood on his shirt. There was probably blood splatter on Mickey's shoes too, but he stopped following the blood trail.

Made himself stop.

"George…"

"What's happened?"

As if he truly wanted to be told what he already knew he didn't want to hear.

"Your friend Beth…," Mickey got out before Leeta darted around the corner, robe swirling behind her.

"Don't believe him! Whatever he's telling you, don't believe the bastard!"

George reached out, grabbed for her, missed. The first slap might have taken Mickey by surprise, but the second Mickey simply allowed.

"I'm sorry, Leeta."

"The fuck you're sorry! Get out of here! Leave us alone!"

He succeeded in catching one of his wife's arms, pulled her back, part of him wanting that fight, the Mickey/Leeta wrangle, to go on and on because once it ended there'd only be revelation.

"Leeta," he said. "Stop. Stop. Something's happened to Beth."

"What are you talking about?"

If she hadn't seen the blood smears before, she saw them now. From both of them, for an instant, she jerked away, drew in her arms, her shoulders.

Then again she started swinging.

"No! This isn't about Beth. He doesn't know fuck-all about Beth. This is about me. He's come to tell you about me!"

"I saw the taillights, got across the ditch, to her car, but…I'm sorry," Mickey said. "There was nothing I could do by then. She was already gone."

"No. No! Liar!" Leeta screamed, withdrawing farther into the room's darkness. "You're lying to get back at me!"

"Leeta, I swear to you, to both of you, this isn't about anything but finding your friend on Swampside."

He had no idea why Mickey swore to such a thing or felt he had to. He had no idea why Beth had been on Swampside, a racer's highway.

"Beth's fine!" Leeta screamed behind him. "Make him say it, George! Make him!"

When Mickey motioned him into the yard, he dumbly followed.

The porch light revealed a paste of bug guts and grit on the windshield and front grille of Mickey's sports car.

Standing alongside bug massacre, he'd hear the rest.

"I'm almost sure the impact killed her," Mickey said. "I don't think she…suffered."

He nodded.

At the speculation that Beth hadn't, in the end, suffered? Acknowledging Mickey's qualifications to judge Beth's pain or lack thereof in the driver's seat of the smashed Plymouth?

"But there's something else you probably should hear now—before you hear it later."

Meaning the bad news hadn't stopped coming. There'd only been a pause, a brief intermission, before bad news joined bad news, turning the whole of it worse. But what could be worse than dead and gone and never coming back?

"There weren't any skid marks," Mickey said. "No other cars were involved. She hit the tree square on."

Through "hit the tree square on" his head kept up its horrible, automatic nodding, as if he agreed with what he was hearing, accepted it, understood it. As if any of it made sense.

"Maybe you want to tell Leeta, maybe not. The cops will know. So word will get around," Mickey said.

To busy his mouth, distract his brain from the conclusion Mickey Waterman had so obviously reached, he asked: "Where exactly on Swampside?"

As if a precise location would give him the evidence he needed to deny that Beth had intentionally set out to harm herself.

"About three miles short of the state line," Mickey answered.

If he stood long enough in the heavy night air, maybe someone other than Mickey would arrive with a different version. There'd been an accident—serious, but not fatal. Beth had been taken to the hospital with treatable wounds, healable injuries, all visitors welcome. And with that more cheerful report, he'd go in, assure Leeta: a close call, but nothing damaged that couldn't be repaired, nothing broken that couldn't be mended.

Again Mickey Waterman apologized: for being the messenger, for not being able to save the dead. The hand offered was flecked with grass and Beth's dried blood. But George shook it. He shook it.

"If there's anything I can do—for you or Leeta," Mickey said. "Anything. Name it."

"I appreciate that you came to tell us"—the most absurd statement of his life.

How could he appreciate being told Beth had died and meant to?

Through the screen door, he saw Leeta pacing, telephone cord stretched, receiver to her ear. Chewing her nails and pacing.

When he walked in, she held up a wet finger in warning.

"She's just drunk. You know she never answers when she's drunk."

"Leeta," he said, and she said: "Don't! Don't! Just give her another minute. She just needs another minute to get to the....goddamn it, Beth! Pick up your goddamn phone!"

He found his way to the couch.

Across the room, on top of the TV, two framed photographs. One of him and Leeta, armored in prom night finery, smiling stiffly. Next to it, less in focus, a photo of him and Leeta and Beth. At the end of a day of beach carousing, Beth had insisted on a "trio shot." Extending her camera arm, she'd clicked blind, capturing his burnt nose, Leeta's wind-whipped hair, her own wide open mouth. She'd been laughing. They'd all been laughing.

Leeta slammed down the phone. Picked it up again.

The porch light was still on. He'd turned it on to talk with Mickey, forgotten to turn it off after their talking was done.

If he flipped the switch now, as soon as he did, he'd be giving what had been visible back over to darkness.

He couldn't do that any more than he could make himself go over to the trailer in the dead of night.

He'd wait for daylight.

He'd sit and wait.

The road at dawn was empty of tourists and farmers, empty even of possums. Driving through Celus Snowden's field and into the trailer's yard, George used the Jeep's lowest gear, respectful of the morning's quiet and quieter dead. But walking toward the trailer, he became, suddenly, the noisiest creature on earth.

His heavy brogans, his loud breath.

Even turning the door handle disturbed the peace.

The trailer wasn't locked. He didn't have to break in. But once inside, regardless, he felt like a trespassing stranger: nothing looked or smelled the way it had when Beth lived here.

No cans or cartons or bottles on the counters or tabletops. No record stack on the couch. The kitchen sink had been scrubbed; the sink trap, cleared. The soles of his shoes stuck to the mopped linoleum.

There were no towels in the bathroom. The medicine cabinet was bare. Metal hooks dangled from the shower rod but no shower curtain.

In the bedroom, the bed had been stripped. Nothing remained in the closets or chest of drawers.

He sat on the mattress, sank with it.

There was a clock on the bedside table but it wasn't ticking. It had stopped charting time at ten past four.

Before leaving, Beth hadn't rewound her clock because she hadn't meant to come back: to the trailer, to this bed. Hadn't intended, ever again, to wake up, go to work, play softball, drink at Graff's, celebrate birthdays.

Done with hanging out in the middle of a cornfield.

Done with growing older, growing old.

Finished with work, play, friends, enemies, Mawatuck.

Finished with the winding and rewinding of clocks.

Finished with Leeta, finished with him.

Finished with life.

They'd lost her.

How could he and Leeta have lost Beth too?

When the drunk theory became impossible to sustain, Leeta invented other denials. An unannounced elopement. Matt and Beth, those sneaks, just took off, left for their honeymoon without telling anyone. Who knew where they'd gone?

"Maybe Miami Beach? Doesn't that sound like somewhere Beth would want to go? I think it does. Don't you, George? Don't you?"

But then the supposed bridegroom showed up alone on their doorstep with his own attempt to explain what none of them could.

Red-faced and stoical, Matt Spruill declared that he'd meant to have the Plymouth's brakes checked; that he'd long suspected the pads had worn thin. A hundred times, Matt Spruill said, he'd thought about setting up that safety inspection. But he'd put it off. And now he'd never forgive himself.

For the graveside-only service, the hearse and its occupants travelled the narrow field path; all others had to park on the shoulder of 178 and walk in.

Unlike the fence surrounding the Scaff dead, the Anderson graveyard fence was wooden and painted white.

Too late George realized he should have volunteered to mow the grass inside the Anderson graveyard. He could have contributed that service. But he hadn't thought to offer, had given no thought to graveyard grass until he stood outside it, facing Beth's casket.

Only Beth's Aunt Grace and the preacher stood beneath the green tarp. There were no flowers on the casket, no flowered wreaths. Aunt Grace had forbidden frivolous blooming flowers. Gloved hands folded, with a disapproving eye, Aunt Grace looked out upon them, sinners in the field.

The president of Mawatuck Savings, Beth's coworkers, Sandy Walker, the softball team, the bartender at Graff's, Tommy Constantine, everyone who had helped celebrate Beth's final birthday, including Mickey Waterman and Rebecca Denby—all solemnly gathered at the grave of the unexpectedly dead.

Everything seemed stable until it wasn't.

Everything seemed solid until it cracked.

Those were lessons the son of a fatalistic father should have learned while still teething, yet he'd refused, continued to refuse, to anticipate and prepare for the bad that could and did repeatedly happen.

Matt Spruill attended in full military dress. Supremely disciplined, even in sadness, Matt Spruill stood with his knees locked, arms braced.

Leeta wore the darkest dress she owned, a deep maroon, spotted with mildew. She'd forgotten to apply makeup or decided against wearing any. Rarely had he seen her face so naked. Before they'd left the house, he'd wiped her fingernails with a napkin, she'd let him wipe them, but almost immediately the tortured quick began to bleed again.

He wore his blue wedding suit, the only suit he owned, wide of cuff and lapel. Appearing in it, he'd expected an argument about clothes, but Leeta had said nothing about what he wore, about anything, dressing herself in such haphazard, last minute fashion, he hadn't realized she was ready when she was.

To help her out of the Mustang, passenger side, he'd offered his arm. The road's shoulder sloped sharply. She accepted the support, leaned hard into his chest. In all their years together, he'd never felt such dependence from her, never felt so much her mainstay. And now he did. Because Beth was gone. Because there were only the two of them.

Quoting passages from the Book of Job, the preacher chastised the feebleness of man's faith, the puniness of human resolve.

Let the stars of the dawn be dark; let the morning wait in vain for the light.

For man is born to trouble, as the sparks fly upward.

And Job said: Yes, yes. I have heard such things. You are all miserable comforters. If I speak my sorrow is not lessened, and if I do not speak, does it leave?

At the conclusion of the service, Aunt Grace set off down the field path alone. Without her vigilant guarding, a queue formed around the casket.

Because Leeta didn't move, he didn't move either.

Mickey came to them. Again George shook the hand offered.

"I'm very sorry for your loss," Rebecca Denby said—first to Leeta, then to him.

Leeta didn't acknowledge their presence, the condolence, didn't react when Stella Wallace passed by, whispering about a deserted road, no second car in the second lane.

In groups of twos and threes, Beth's mourners departed.

"Leeta," he urged. "Leeta."

"I can't," she said. "I can't leave."

But to stay and watch Mawatuck dirt rain down on Beth's casket? Dirt he used to love?

The hearse departed. The shovels and shovelers arrived.

Matt Spruill took off his dress hat to kiss the casket but put it back on to walk away.

"Leeta," he said, the sky dimming above them. "Leeta."

"Please, George," she said. "Not yet. Because as soon as I turn around and walk away it will be like admitting she's really in that box. Like I'm really saying goodbye."

To argue otherwise would mean he believed some part of Beth had survived the crash, the morgue, the crating in a casket; that she'd been released from misery; that she'd moved on to a better, timeless place. And he believed none of that. He felt the same as Leeta. As soon as they turned around, turned their backs, they'd lose everything that remained of Beth. Even the coffin that held her would disappear underground. In a week, two weeks, there'd be a granite marker and grass that needed cutting again. Only granite and grass.

He reached for one of Leeta's tortured hands.

Side by side, heels dug in among corn shucks, they stayed on. They stayed and made Beth's buriers wait.

* * *

Revealed by the Plymouth's headlights: racer marks.

A sign, a signal, racer marks.

Get on with it. Finish up.

With resolution came company: a tuxedoed passenger in the passenger seat.

Not pleased, the tuxedo.

With Beth.

With her intent.

"I take absolutely no responsibility for this circus," He said.

Then He and His cigarette vanished.

He could have stuck around.

She remembered their common revulsion.

Did He imagine she'd forgotten?

Did He assume she'd embarrass both of them by writhing and moaning, flailing and sobbing?

He should have known better.

By this late hour He should have known her.

Approaching the sharpest Swampside curve she pushed flat the accelerator, lifted her hands from the steering wheel.

The tires quit asphalt; the Plymouth soared.

But the levitation didn't fool her.

A rooted pine tree was her true destination.

She saw that solid trunk of wood coming at her, welcomed it.

What ended her ended melancholy, ended grief.

Glory be to the pine tree.

Kat Meads is the author of 16 books and chapbooks of prose and poetry, including: *2:12 a.m.; Not Waving; For You, Madam Lenin; Little Pockets of Alarm; The Invented Life of Kitty Duncan; Sleep*; and a mystery novel written under the pseudonym Z.K. Burrus. She has received a National Endowment for the Arts Fellowship, a California Artist Fellowship, two Silicon Valley artist grants and artist residencies at the Fine Arts Work Center in Provincetown, Yaddo, Millay Colony, Dorland, and the Montalvo Center for the Arts. Other prizes include the *Chelsea* award for fiction, the *New Letters* award for essay, and the Editors' Choice award from *Drunken Boat*. Her short plays have been produced in New York, Los Angeles, San Francisco and elsewhere. She is a three-time *ForeWord Reviews* Book of the Year finalist, and four of her essays have been selected as Notables in Houghton Mifflin Harcourt's *Best American Essays* series. Her flash fiction collection, *Little Pockets of Alarm*, was runner-up for the University of Massachusetts Press Juniper Prize. Her novel *For You, Madam Lenin* received an IPPY (Independent Publisher Award) Silver Medal and was shortlisted for the Montaigne Medal for thought-provoking literature. Her essay collection *2:12 a.m.* received an IPPY Gold Medal. She has been an invited presenter at conferences on both the East and West Coasts, including the Mendocino Writers Conference, Florida International University's Seaside Writers Conference, East of Eden Writers Conference and the Eastern North Carolina Literary Festival. Reviewers have described her work as "exquisite" (*Historical Novels Review*), "remarkable" (*American Book Review*) "smart and provocative" (*Other Voices*), "bold and beautiful" (*Midwest Book Review*), "riveting" (*New Pages*) and "worth reading for the dialogue alone" (*Greensboro News and Record*). A native of North Carolina, she currently lives in California and teaches in Oklahoma City University's low-residency Red Earth MFA program.

www.ingramcontent.com/pod-product-compliance
Lightning Source LLC
Chambersburg PA
CBHW072349020726
47506CB00004B/1077